Beyond

The Ice

By
KingELOTheGod

EBook ISBN - 979-8-9920291-3-0
Paperback ISBN - 979-8-9920291-4-7
Hard Cover ISBN - 979-8-9920291-5-4

(Isaiah 40:22)
It is he that sits upon the circle of the Earth
And the inhabitants are as grasshoppers.

(Book Description)

When geologist Larry Bridge embarks on a research mission to the frozen heart of Antarctica, he anticipates long days of data collection, icy winds, and isolation. What he doesn't expect is to uncover a world hidden beneath the ice—an ancient city, enigmatic guardians, and a civilization beyond imagination.

As Larry and his team delve deeper into the mysteries of the ice, they encounter Angel, a captivating inhabitant of the Eloran city. Drawn together by a love that transcends worlds, Larry and Angel must navigate the challenges of two civilizations colliding while facing an ancient adversary determined to keep the secrets of the ice buried forever. From harrowing expeditions through deadly blizzards to breathtaking discoveries of advanced technologies and alien wildlife, "Beyond the Ice" is a thrilling journey of survival, love, and hope. With each revelation, Larry and his team are pulled into a greater purpose—

bridging humanity's past and future to forge a new golden age. This epic tale of exploration, resilience, and romance will take readers on a mesmerizing journey into the unknown.

Perfect for fans of speculative fiction and those who dream of uncharted worlds,
"Beyond the Ice" is a story of connection, courage, and the enduring power of love.
Prepare to journey where few have gone before. The ice is calling.

(The Adventure Ahead)

I never thought my senior year of college would take me somewhere like this. Sitting in my cramped dorm room, surrounded by wrinkled notebooks, half-read research articles, and the stale aroma of instant ramen, I stared at my laptop screen. The email's subject line burned into my vision like a beacon: "Expedition Opportunity: Antarctica Research Team." My hands hovered over the keyboard, trembling slightly. I scrolled through the message again, each word jumping out like a bolt of electricity: "Congratulations, Larry Bridge. You've been selected." The message read, so I leaned back in my chair, the springs creaking under my weight. Me. Larry and Antarctica. The thought felt surreal, as if it belonged to someone else. I was just a 22-year-old environmental science major from rural Europe. A young Black man trying to make something of himself in a world that didn't always make it easy.

Antarctica was the stuff of documentaries and adventure stories, not something real people—people like me—did. My reflection in the darkened screen stared back at me, uncertain but resolute. A face framed by short, neatly lined hair and a beard that was still deciding whether it wanted to fully grow in. My dark brown eyes held a question I wasn't sure how to answer: Was I ready for this? I ran a hand over my face, the smoothness of my skin interrupted by the rough stubble. My textbooks and scattered notes offered no reassurance. They just sat there, silent witnesses to the life I was about to leave behind. Dr. Langley, my environmental science professor, had been the one to push me toward this.

"Larry," she'd said, her voice a mix of encouragement and insistence, "your mind sees things differently. You see connections. Patterns. That's exactly what this expedition needs. Don't let doubt stop you from applying."
I smiled politely and muttered something about thinking it over. Later that night, though, I stared at the application for hours. Part of me wanted to close the tab and forget the whole thing. People like me didn't just jet off to Antarctica. But then, wasn't that the point? To break the mold, to prove that I could go beyond the boundaries the world assumed for me? I clicked submit. And now, two months later, here I was.

The week leading up to the trip was a blur. Between packing, finishing finals, and fielding phone calls from my mom, I barely had time to process what was happening. "Larry, are you sure about this?" she asked during one call. Her voice, warm and familiar, carried an edge of concern. "It's... Antarctica, baby. That's not just cold—it's cold cold. "You've never even been skiing!" "I know, Mom," I said, forcing a laugh. "But I'll be fine. They'll have all the gear. And

1

professionals. It's not like I'm just wandering out there with a pair of mittens and a scarf." She wasn't convinced. "You'd better call me as soon as you can. Or email. Or... whatever you can do out there." "I promise, Mom," I said.

By the time I boarded the first flight to Punta Arenas, Chile, my nerves were stretched thin. The long-haul flight was just the beginning of my journey to the bottom of the world. The plane was a packed 777, filled with tourists, researchers, and the odd mix of people who seemed to exist only in airports. I settled into my seat, a cramped spot next to the window. A small mercy—it gave me a view of the clouds and something to focus on other than the gnawing anxiety in my chest. The first few hours passed in a haze of in-flight announcements, the hum of the engines, and the rhythmic clinking of drink carts. I tried to distract myself with a book, but the words blurred together. Eventually, I gave up and stared out the window. Somewhere over the Gulf of Mexico as it was once called, I struck up a conversation with the man sitting beside me, a burly geologist named Tom. He had the kind of booming voice and hearty laugh that filled a room. "First time heading south?" he asked after I'd introduced myself. "Yeah," I admitted. "Is it that obvious?" Tom chuckled. "A little. But don't worry, you'll be fine. Just remember: Antarctica's not like anything you've ever seen. Beautiful and brutal all at once." He launched into a story about his last trip there, describing how a sudden whiteout storm had trapped his team in their tents for 36 hours. His words painted a vivid picture of the challenges ahead, but his tone carried an undercurrent of reverence for the icy continent.

After a layover in Santiago, the final leg to Punta Arenas felt more real. The plane grew quieter as researchers began reviewing notes and adjusting equipment in the overhead compartments. By the time we touched down, I was exhausted but buzzing with anticipation. Punta Arenas felt like the edge of the world. The wind was relentless, whipping through the narrow streets and carrying with it the salty tang of the sea. I stayed overnight, catching a few hours of restless sleep before boarding the smaller plane to King George Island the next morning. This was the flight I'd been warned about. The plane was loud, the seats uncomfortably close, and every bump of turbulence felt exaggerated. The hum of the engines made conversation difficult, so I was left with my thoughts.

The hours dragged on. The view outside shifted from the deep blue of open ocean to the brilliant white of endless ice. It was hypnotic, almost dreamlike. I watched as we crossed over jagged mountain ranges buried beneath snow, the peaks catching the sunlight and scattering it like shards of glass. Somewhere halfway through the flight, the reality of what I was doing sank in. This wasn't just a school project or an internship. This was the edge of human exploration, a place where survival depended on skill, preparation, and maybe a little luck.

The woman next to me must have noticed my expression, because she leaned over and said, "First time heading to the ice?" I nodded. "Yeah. Guess I'm not hiding it very well." "You're fine," she said, smiling. "I'm Sarah by the way a Marine biologist." "Larry," I replied. "a Environmental science major." She nodded approvingly. "Well, Larry, let me give you some advice. Always double-check your layers, never underestimate the cold, and if you see a penguin, give it space. They look cute, but they bite." Her easy confidence was contagious, and I felt some of my tension ease. When the plane finally touched down, the cold hit me like a wall. Even with all my layers, it was a shock—an instant reminder that I was stepping into a place where nature reigned supreme. Dr. Alan Harrison, the team leader, greeted us with a firm handshake and a no-nonsense attitude. "Welcome to King George Island," he said. "You've got an hour to settle in before the briefing. Stay on schedule, and we'll get along just fine."

The first night in the research station was eerily silent, yet my mind refused to quiet down. Even though exhaustion weighed on my body like a lead blanket, sleep remained elusive. The events of the day replayed over and over in my head—the long, grueling flight, stepping onto Antarctic soil for the first time, and the overwhelming presence of the station itself. But something else gnawed at me beneath the surface, an inexplicable feeling that I had been chosen for this mission for reasons beyond my understanding.

I had hoped that a little rest would put those thoughts to bed, but my bladder had other plans. Groaning, I peeled myself from the warmth of my cot, grabbed my jacket, and stepped into the dimly lit corridor of the station. The hallway was quiet, save for the faint hum of the station's heating system. I trudged toward the bathroom, my breath fogging slightly in the cold air despite the controlled climate. As I reached the door, I caught something unusual—a low murmur of voices from further down the hall.

At first, I ignored it. It was late, and I figured maybe a few of the researchers were still up, chatting about the day. But something about their hushed tones unsettled me. It wasn't casual conversation. It was secretive. Deliberate. Curiosity got the best of me. And instead of continuing to the bathroom, I crept closer to the sound, keeping my footsteps as silent as possible. The voices were coming from a small operations room just off the main hallway. The door was cracked open, and through the sliver of space, I could see the faint glow of a computer screen casting eerie shadows on the walls. I held my breath and listened.

"...I still can't believe they drafted us into the CIA just like that," one voice said, hushed but urgent.

"We didn't exactly have a choice," another responded. "We were selected, and now we're in. This mission is bigger than we thought." My stomach tightened. The CIA? What the hell were they talking about? I had signed up for a research expedition, not some covert government operation. A third voice, one I recognized as Dr. Alan Harrison's, the leader of our team, spoke next. "Keep your voices down. If anyone finds out, we're screwed. The agency handpicked us for a reason. And Larry… he's part of it, whether he knows it or not." I froze. Me?

There was a brief pause before someone asked, "Are we sure about him? He doesn't seem like he knows anything." "That's the point," Dr. Alan Harrison answered. "He was chosen specifically because he doesn't. But the agency wants him here. That's why we got clearance to operate beyond the normal Antarctic boundaries. This mission isn't just about research—it's about discovery. And when the time comes, he'll play his role." I felt my pulse pounding in my ears. What role? What exactly had I been thrown into? I wanted to burst into the room and demand answers, but every instinct in my body screamed at me to stay hidden. This was something I was never meant to hear. If they knew I had been eavesdropping, I had no idea what they would do.

So carefully, I took a step back, making sure not to make a sound. I retraced my steps to the bathroom, my mind racing a million miles a second. I splashed cold water on my face, staring at my reflection in the cracked mirror. The CIA had orchestrated this whole thing and I wasn't here by accident. Then a sick feeling settled in my gut, but I forced myself to stay calm. I couldn't let them know I had heard. Not yet. So for the rest of the night, I laid in bed staring at the ceiling, wide awake, and I knew that this was it and my adventure was truly ahead of me now, and whatever challenges waited in the icy expanse, I was ready to face them.

(The Dream Team)

The next morning the first thing that I noticed when I walked through the research station was that during the day there was a hum. It's subtle but constant—an orchestra of generators, heaters, and computers working overtime to keep the station alive in the middle of nowhere. And that hum reminds you you're not in the real world anymore. You're in Antarctica. And by the time I set foot in the station after that long night when I arrived, the rest of the team had already settled into their roles. Walking into a tightly knit group as the new guy is never easy, but here, on the edge of the world, it felt especially daunting. Dr. Sarah Conway was the first to greet me. She met me at the airstrip, a warm smile cutting through the icy wind.

"You must be Larry," she said, her voice almost lost to the gusts. "Welcome to paradise." I laughed, though I wasn't sure if it was at her joke or out of sheer relief. She helped me haul my gear into the station, chatting the whole way. Her easygoing nature was disarming, and by the time we stepped inside, I felt a little less like an intruder. Inside, the station was a labyrinth of narrow hallways and low ceilings, and every inch of it designed for function over comfort. The walls were covered with maps, safety instructions, and fading photos of past expeditions. It smelled of coffee, cleaning supplies, and something metallic that I couldn't quite place.

"This is home," Sarah said, gesturing to the central corridor. "For better or worse." Dinner on my 2nd night was my official introduction to the team. We gathered in the common room, a surprisingly cozy space considering the rest of the station's utilitarian vibe. A long table dominated the room, surrounded by mismatched chairs. The walls were plastered with flags, signatures, and notes left by previous teams—a patchwork quilt of memories and milestones. Dr. Alan Harrison, the expedition leader, sat at the head of the table. He had the kind of presence that commanded respect without him needing to say much. His sharp blue eyes scanned me as I introduced myself, and he gave a small nod.

"Glad you made it," he said simply. The rest of the team introduced themselves in turn. There was Tom Rourke, the geologist, whose handshake was as steady as his personality. Dr. Elena Morales, the glaciologist, gave me a quick nod and a polite smile before returning her attention to her plate. Drew Miller, the field technician, was the opposite—grinning as he leaned back in his chair and launched into a story about how he once fixed a snowmobile with duct tape and a pack of gum. "You'll like it here," Drew said, smirking. "Well, assuming you don't mind the cold. Or the isolation. Or the constant threat of frostbite." "Don't scare him off," Sarah said, rolling her eyes. The conversation shifted to lighter topics, but I stayed quiet, taking it all in. These were people who had been to the edge of the world and came back with stories to tell. I felt out of place, like a kid trying to sit at the grown-ups' table.

But over the next few days, I started to find my footing—or at least, I tried to. The station operated like a well-oiled machine, with everyone moving purposefully through their routines. Mornings began early, with breakfast in the common room. Coffee was the lifeblood of the station, and the pot never seemed to run dry. Conversations over oatmeal and powdered eggs ranged from the day's tasks to the latest satellite data. "Another storm rolling in," Dr. Harrison would say, his voice calm but firm. "We'll need to adjust our schedule."

After my official introduction to the research team, I was still getting my bearings. The research station hummed with life, an intricate mix of mechanical noises and human interaction. I had spent most of the morning adjusting to the rhythm of the station. Each team member seemed to know their role and moved with a sense of purpose. Still, I couldn't shake the memory of the hushed conversation I'd overheard the previous night. The cryptic mention of the CIA drafting the team and choosing me specifically for this mission hung in my mind like an ominous cloud. I had resolved to act normal—pretending nothing was out of the ordinary—but my ears were now attuned to anything that sounded remotely suspicious.

Then after lunch, I wandered the halls, eager to explore the station further. I tried to keep it casual, sticking to the areas I was officially allowed to access. The researchers had mentioned a greenhouse and an observatory on my tour, but I hadn't seen them yet. I decided to go looking for those. While roaming the corridors, I passed by a door labeled "Storage C." I paid it no mind at first—it looked like just another supply closet. But as I walked past, I caught a faint sound: voices.

I stopped dead in my tracks. The voices were muffled, but the tone carried weight, urgency. My pulse quickened. Another meeting? In broad daylight this time? My mind raced, wondering if this had anything to do with what I'd overheard last night. I looked around. The hallway was empty. Carefully, I leaned closer to the door, trying to make out the words. "...security protocols are already in place," a voice said. I recognized it as Dr. Alan Harrison's, the team leader. "We're not here to question the directive, we're here to execute it." Another voice chimed in, softer but no less firm. "But what about him? Larry doesn't even know what he's been brought into. How long are we supposed to keep him in the dark?" They were talking about me. My stomach tightened as I pressed myself closer to the wall, my heart thundering in my chest.

The air around me seemed to thin. "Look," Dr. Alan Harrison said, his tone sharper now. "You've read the briefing. He was handpicked for a reason. We don't have to like it, but it's not our call. Our job is to keep him focused on the cover story. Do you want to explain to the Agency why we failed? Because I don't." There was a pause, and then another voice spoke—this time it sounded like one of the engineers, Elena. "I get that, but we're walking a fine line here. This isn't a small operation. If he finds out, if he figures out the real purpose of this mission, it could compromise everything. Especially if he reacts badly." There was a low hum of murmured agreement before Dr. Alan Harrison spoke again. "We'll deal with that if it happens. For now, we stick to the plan. No deviations. Understood?" There was a chorus of quiet "yes" responses. I stepped back from the door, my breathing shallow. My thoughts were a storm of confusion and unease. The real purpose of the mission? A cover story? What in the world had I been thrown into? I wanted to march into that room and demand answers again, but instinct still told me that was a terrible idea. They had mentioned the CIA again. This wasn't just some Antarctic research project. This was something bigger—something they weren't telling me.

So I slowly backed away, careful not to make any noise. My feet carried me down the hallway almost on autopilot, though I had no idea where I was headed. But by the time I reached an empty common area, I leaned against a wall, trying to catch my breath. I replayed the conversation in my head, analyzing every word. It was clear that I wasn't just another researcher here by coincidence. My presence was part of some larger plan, and the team knew it. Worse, they were in on it. But why me? Why had I been chosen? And what exactly was the mission's true purpose? The weight of these questions pressed down on me, but I made a decision right then and there: if they thought I was just some clueless tagalong, they were wrong. I wasn't going to confront them yet, but I also wasn't going to sit back and wait for the truth to reveal itself. From now on, I'd pay close attention to everything—every conversation, every movement. If there were secrets to uncover, I'd find them.

So by the time the day started to end, I had resolved to play the role of the naïve newcomer. If they were watching me, I'd make sure I gave them nothing to suspect. But inside, I was already piecing together a plan. Whatever was going on here, I wasn't going to let it blindside me. So the rest of the day was a blur of activity. Sarah spent most of her time in the lab, analyzing water samples and reviewing footage from underwater drones. She had a way of making even the most tedious tasks seem interesting, often narrating her work like a nature documentary. "Look at this," she said on that afternoon, holding up a vial of water. "To most people, it's just water. But to us? It's a story. A glimpse into the life that thrives in the harshest conditions." Tom, on the other hand, was more reserved. I often found him hunched over a microscope or a core sample, his brow furrowed in concentration. He'd explain his findings if I asked, his voice steady and deliberate, like he was telling a bedtime story. Drew's workspace was a chaotic corner of the station filled with tools, wires, and half-assembled gadgets. He was the problem-solver, always tinkering with something.

"Antarctica doesn't care about your plans," he told me once. "Something will break, and when it does, you better know how to fix it." Then there was Elena. She was a paradox—intensely focused yet distant, as if her mind was always elsewhere. I once asked her about the glacier models she was working on, and she launched into a detailed explanation that left my head spinning. "Sorry," she said afterward, offering a rare smile. "I get carried away." Then after a long day of prep work, I found myself alone in the common room with Dr. Harrison. He was reviewing a stack of papers, his reading glasses perched on his nose. "How are you settling in?" he asked without looking up. "Good," I said, though the word felt insufficient. "It's... a lot to take in." He set the papers down and looked at me, his expression unreadable. "It's not an easy place to be, Larry. But you're here for a reason. Remember that."

His words stuck with me. This wasn't just a research expedition—it was a mission, a collective effort to understand and preserve one of the planet's last frontiers. And I was a part of it. And by the time my third day on the ice arrived, I felt more prepared, though the nerves were still there. The team had accepted me into their ranks, and I was beginning to see how each piece of the puzzle fitted together. This wasn't just a group of scientists—it was a family. A family bound not by blood, but by a shared purpose and a willingness to endure the harshest conditions for the sake of discovery. So as I lay in my bunk that night, listening to the wind howl outside, I thought about the journey that had brought me here. The sacrifices, the doubts, the excitement—it all led to this moment. Tomorrow, I'd step onto the ice for the first time for real. And I couldn't wait to see what it had to teach me.

(Frozen Frontiers)

On the next day the cold was the first thing I noticed when I stepped outside the research station that morning. Even through the layers of insulated clothing, it wrapped around me like an invisible force, biting at every exposed inch of skin. The research station, a collection of metal prefabricated buildings perched on the edge of King George Island, looked like a cluster of misplaced shipping containers against the endless expanse of white. I pulled my goggles down to shield my face from the cutting wind, which roared across the ice like an angry ghost. The air tasted sharp and clean, with a purity I had never experienced before. It was hard to believe that such a vast, desolate place could hold so much life in its icy grip—or so many secrets.

"Ready to see what the ice has to offer?" Sarah asked, walking up beside me. She carried a clipboard and an energy I envied at this early hour. "Ready as I'll ever be," I said, trying to match her enthusiasm. The day began with a safety briefing in the central building. Dr. Harrison, our no-nonsense expedition leader, stood at the head of the room, a map of the region spread out on the table in front of him. The others—geologists, biologists, climatologists, and a handful of other specialists—gathered around, some sipping coffee, others already buried in notebooks. Dr. Harrison's voice was steady, commanding. "Today, we'll split into teams and head out to the glacier. The primary goal is to collect core samples, water data, and initial environmental readings. Remember, this isn't just about science. It's about survival. No one wanders off, no one ignores the protocols. Because out here, one mistake could cost you your life."

His words sank in like ice melting into my veins. The gravity of being in a place so unforgiving hit me. This wasn't just an adventure—it was a test. An hour later, I found myself in a convoy of snowmobiles roaring across the frozen tundra. The landscape stretched endlessly in every direction, a vast, unbroken sea of ice punctuated by jagged peaks and the occasional dark patch where the wind had swept the snow away. I sat behind Tom on his snowmobile, clutching the side rails as the vehicle bumped and swayed over the uneven terrain. He turned his head slightly to shout over the engine noise. "Beautiful, isn't it?" he said, his voice muffled by the wind. "Yeah," I managed, though the word felt inadequate. Beautiful didn't quite capture the alien majesty of this place. The cold seeped in despite my heavy gear. My gloves felt too thin, and my toes had already gone numb inside my insulated boots. The wind found every gap, slipping past my scarf and under my hood. I focused on the rhythm of the snowmobile, its engine's steady vibration a small comfort against the unforgiving elements.

Sarah and Dr. Harrison rode ahead, their figures reduced to silhouettes against the endless white. Behind us, two more snowmobiles followed, each laden with equipment and supplies. Tom pointed to a jagged ridge in the distance. "That's the edge of the glacier. We'll set up base just below it." When we arrived, the glacier loomed like a frozen mountain, its surface a chaotic maze of ridges and crevasses. The ice glinted under the weak sunlight, a kaleidoscope of blues and whites that seemed almost alive. "Welcome to one of nature's greatest time capsules," Dr. Harrison said as he dismounted his snowmobile. "This ice has been here for tens of thousands of years. It holds the history of the Earth itself." The team sprang into action, unloading equipment and setting up a temporary base. Portable weather stations were assembled, and core drilling rigs were prepared. Every movement was precise and deliberate, the efficiency of experienced professionals.

Then I was assigned to help Sarah collect water samples from a nearby melt stream that snaked through the glacier. The stream's surface was a mirror of ice, the water beneath it so clear that it seemed invisible. "Careful," Sarah said as we approached. "The ice here can be thin. Follow my lead." I nodded, my boots crunching against the frost-covered surface. The sound of the glacier was eerie— low groans and cracks that seemed to come from deep within the earth. Sarah demonstrated how to lower a sampling device into the water without disturbing the sediment. Her movements were confident, almost graceful, despite the bulky gloves and heavy coat. "Your turn," she said, handing me the device. I took it carefully, my hands trembling—not just from the cold, but from the weight of the task. Lowering it into the water, I watched as the sample container filled, the icy liquid shimmering like liquid glass. "Not bad," Sarah said, her approval warming me more than the layers of clothing ever could. As the day wore on, the temperature dropped, and the wind picked up. The light shifted, casting long shadows across the glacier. The team worked tirelessly, their movements synchronized like a well-rehearsed dance.

At one point, Tom called me over to help set up a weather station. The device was a complex array of sensors and antennas designed to measure everything from temperature and wind speed to atmospheric pressure. "Hold this steady," he said, handing me a metal pole that felt like ice against my gloves. Together, we secured the station, the wind fighting us every step of the way. When we finally stepped back to admire our work, Tom clapped me on the back. "Not bad for a rookie," he said with a grin. The return journey was quieter, the team subdued by exhaustion. The sun dipped lower, painting the ice in shades of pink and gold. I leaned back against the snowmobile's seat, my body aching but my mind racing. Back at the station, the mood was lighter. People shared stories over steaming mugs of coffee, and their laughter a sharp contrast to the stark silence of the glacier. "First day on the ice," Sarah said, raising her mug in a mock toast. "How do you feel, Larry?" "Tired," I admitted, "but... good. Like I'm part of something bigger." She smiled. "You are." That night, lying in my bunk, I stared at the ceiling, my mind replaying the day's events. The ice, the wind, the sense of stepping into a world untouched by time—it was overwhelming and exhilarating all at once. And the wind howled outside, a reminder of the relentless power of this place. And yet, beneath the fear and fatigue, there was a flicker of something else: excitement.

But later that night after our first official day on the ice, I found myself exhausted, yet unable to fall asleep. The day had been a whirlwind of sensory overload—alien winds biting through my parka, the haunting stillness of the frozen expanse, and the weight of an unshakable feeling that this mission was far from ordinary. I laid on the small cot in my room, staring up at the ceiling, and the hum of the heater was the only sound breaking the eerie silence of the research station. And the isolation of Antarctica had a way of magnifying every small creak and groan in the building, each sound hinting at something more than just the mundane.

My mind had been replaying every interaction with the team. There was something peculiar about them, something unspoken that hinted at a deeper connection they shared despite them being in the C.I.A—but one that I was somehow excluded from. I shook the thought away, chalking it up to first-day jitters and my imagination running wild. But as I closed my eyes, a sudden knock at my door jolted me upright. Before I could respond, the door creaked open, and one by one, the team members filtered into my room. They looked different in the dim light—serious, almost solemn. Sarah, who had been jovial and welcoming earlier, now wore a grave expression. Elena, who usually had a glint of humor in her eyes, looked down at the floor as if avoiding my gaze. Even Dr. Alan Harrison, whose calm demeanor had been a steadying presence, seemed tense, his arms crossed tightly over his chest.

"Uh, everything okay guys?" I asked hesitantly, sitting up. Then Drew closed the door behind him, leaning his back against it as though ensuring no one else could enter or hear. Elena pulled the only chair in the room closer to the cot and sat down, while the rest of the team stood, forming an almost semi-circle around me. "Larry," Dr. Alan Harrison began, his voice low but firm, "we need to talk." My heart began to pound. "What's going on?" For a moment, no one answered. They exchanged glances, a silent conversation passing between them. Finally, Drew sighed heavily and spoke. "We owe you the truth, Larry," he said. "You probably already suspect that this mission isn't what it seems. Well, you're right." I blinked, my throat dry. "What do you mean?" Elena leaned forward, her voice softer but just as serious. "This research mission—it's not just about studying the ice, Larry. It's... bigger than that. We're part of something larger. Something classified." "Classified?" My mind raced, the weight of the word sinking in. Dr. Alan Harrison nodded. "We're on a covert C.I.A. operation."

For a second, I thought I hadn't heard him right. "Wait, what? The C.I.A.? Why would they send a bunch of scientists to Antarctica? What's going on here?" Drew raised a hand to calm me. "We're not just scientists, Larry. We were recruited because of our expertise, yes, but also because of our ability to operate in... unconventional circumstances." "And you," Elena added, her gaze locking onto mine, "were handpicked by the agency for this mission." The room seemed to tilt for a moment. I shook my head, trying to process what they were saying. "Me? Handpicked by the C.I.A.? That doesn't make any sense. I'm just a researcher—" "You're not 'just' anything," Dr. Alan Harrison interrupted. "Your record speaks for itself. Your work, your background—" "Your resilience," then Drew cut in. "The agency saw something in you. They didn't share the specifics with us, but you were chosen for a reason. This operation was too important to leave to chance."

My mind flashed back to the overheard conversations, the secretive tone of their discussions. It all started clicking into place, yet the questions only multiplied. "Why didn't anyone tell me? Why keep me in the dark?" then Elena sighed. "Standard protocol. Need-to-know basis. They didn't want to overwhelm you before you even arrived here. But after today—after seeing how well you handled the ice—we all agreed you deserved to know the truth."

"And what truth is that?" I asked, my voice steadier now, though my pulse was still racing.

Dr. Alan Harrison's expression softened. "This isn't just about studying ice samples or climate data. Antarctica holds secrets, Larry. Secrets that could change the course of human history. We're here to uncover those secrets, but we're not the only ones who know they exist. That's why the C.I.A. is involved. They want to ensure that whatever we find doesn't fall into the wrong hands." Then the room fell silent. My mind was a storm of thoughts, each one louder than the last. "So... all of you knew this from the start? You've been working with the C.I.A. this whole time?" of course I already knew but I was playing my part.

Drew nodded. "We've been operating as a team under their directive. And now, you're part of that team too." "Why tell me now?" I asked, my voice quieter. "Because you've proven yourself," Elena said. "You handled today's challenges without hesitation. You're not just here to fill a role, Larry. You're here because you belong here."

I leaned back against the wall, my head spinning. Part of me wanted to demand more answers, but another part of me knew they wouldn't—or couldn't—say more. There was a weight in the air, a sense of responsibility that I hadn't felt before. "Okay," I finally said, my voice firmer now. "What happens next?" Drew smiled faintly. "We keep going, as a team. But from here on out, Larry, you're in the loop. No more secrets."

The tension in the room seemed to lift, though my thoughts remained heavy. As the team left my room one by one, I lay back down, staring at the ceiling again. The heater hummed softly, but now the sound felt different—less mundane, more purposeful, as if even the station itself was part of something larger. I didn't know what secrets Antarctica held, or why the C.I.A. thought I was the right person for this mission. But one thing was certain: my life had just changed in a way I never could have imagined.

(Whispers Under the Ice)

The next day on the Ice me and the team proceeded as usual and it started as a hum—low, indistinct, like the faint murmur of wind sneaking through the cracks of an ancient cathedral. At first, I thought it was just another auditory illusion of the frozen wilderness. Antarctica, after all, was a land of sensory tricks: horizons blurred by blizzards, light bent through prisms of ice. But this was different. The sound lingered, its vibration subtle but unyielding, like a quiet heartbeat under my boots. Our day began like any other. Breakfast in the cramped station mess hall was a chaotic blend of clattering utensils, muted conversation, and the constant hum of heaters struggling to keep the frigid cold at bay. Despite the comfort of our routine, there was an underlying tension—something none of us wanted to acknowledge out loud.

Dr. Harrison's morning briefing only added to the unease. He stood at the head of the table, his lined face illuminated by the pale glow of the projector. "The shifts we've been monitoring are increasing in frequency," he said, pointing to a series of jagged peaks on a graph. "What does that mean?" Sarah had asked, her voice laced with concern. "It means the ice shelf is unstable," Harrison replied. "More unstable than we anticipated." A heavy silence settled over the room. "But that's why we're here," Harrison continued, his tone firm. "To understand these changes and their implications. We'll proceed with today's assignments as planned, but I want everyone to exercise caution. This environment doesn't forgive mistakes."

The fissures were an hour's trek from the station, and the journey there was anything but easy. The snow beneath our boots shifted unpredictably, sometimes crunching loudly, sometimes absorbing the sound entirely. The sun hung low on the horizon, casting long, distorted shadows across the ice. Sarah walked beside me, her breath fogging the air. "You think Harrison's worried?" she asked. "Worried?" I echoed. "The guy doesn't show much emotion." "Yeah, but did you see his face during the briefing?" she pressed. "He knows something he's not telling us." Tom, walking a few paces ahead, chimed in. "Harrison always knows more than he lets on. That's his thing. But hey, if it's dangerous enough to pack up and leave, I'm all for it. I'm not dying out here." I gave a dry laugh. "And miss out on all this excitement?" Tom smirked but didn't respond.

The fissures came into view suddenly, jagged and otherworldly against the endless expanse of white. They were much larger up close, their edges sharp and menacing. Looking down, I felt a shiver unrelated to the cold. The shadows seemed to twist and shift, as though alive. "Let's get this over with," Sarah said, kneeling to unpack her equipment. We divided the tasks as usual. Sarah set up the data tablet, Tom drilled anchor holes, and I secured the seismic sensors. It was routine, methodical work, but I couldn't shake the unease creeping up my spine. Then I felt it—the vibration. It was faint at first, just a slight tremor under my boots. I paused, thinking it might be the drill, but Tom was still positioning it. The sensation grew stronger, rhythmic, like a pulse. "You guys feel that?" I asked, my voice breaking the silence. Tom frowned, standing up. "Feel what?" "Put your hand on the ice," I said. He crouched, pressing his gloved hand to the surface. After a moment, his eyes widened. "What the hell?" Sarah joined us, her brow furrowed. "It's... it's alive," she murmured. "What do you mean, 'alive'?" Tom asked, his tone laced with sarcasm, though his face betrayed his nerves. Before she could respond, the vibration intensified, accompanied by a low hum. The sound seemed to emanate from the fissures, resonating through the air and the ice alike. "What's causing it?" I asked, my pulse quickening. "Could be geothermal activity," Sarah said, though she didn't sound convinced. "Or something else," Tom muttered.

The hum grew louder, transforming into a deep, resonant drone that seemed to penetrate my very bones. It wasn't just sound—it was something more, something that defied explanation. "Look!" Tom suddenly shouted, pointing toward one of the larger fissures. I followed his gaze and saw it: a faint, pulsating light emanating from deep within the crack. It was subtle at first, a soft glow barely visible against the darkness. But as we watched, it grew brighter, shifting through hues of blue and green like a living aurora. "That's not natural," Sarah whispered, her voice trembling. "Could it be a reflection?" I asked, though I didn't believe it myself. "Of what?" she snapped. Tom stepped closer, peering into the fissure. "Careful!" Sarah warned, but he didn't listen. "What are you doing?" I asked, my heart pounding. "There's... something down there," he said.

The light pulsed rhythmically, in perfect harmony with the vibrations. I couldn't look away, captivated by its ethereal beauty—and terrified by its implications. The crackle of static broke the trance, followed by Harrison's voice. "Team Two, report. What's your status?" Sarah grabbed the radio, her hands shaking. "We're... we're fine. But we've found something unusual." "Define 'unusual,'" Harrison said sharply. "There's a vibration coming from the fissures," she said, struggling to keep her voice steady. "And... there's light. Pulsing light." A long pause followed. Then Harrison's voice returned, clipped and urgent. "Pack up and return to the station immediately." "But—" "Now!" he snapped. We didn't argue. The hum and light remained as we hastily packed our equipment, their presence almost mocking. As we turned to leave, the vibrations seemed to follow us, growing fainter but never entirely fading. The trek back was oppressively silent. None of us spoke, each lost in our thoughts. The light, the hum, the inexplicable sense of being watched—it was too much to process.

Then the station finally came into view, and its warm lights cutting through the encroaching dusk, and I felt an overwhelming sense of relief. But as we stepped inside, the unease didn't fade. Whatever was out there, it wasn't finished with us. And somehow, I knew we'd be going back. A week had passed, but the unease that had settled over our camp after that first encounter with the fissures hadn't dissipated. If anything, it had grown worse. It was as if the ice itself had turned against us—shifting, groaning, whispering secrets we weren't meant to hear. The anomalies were subtle at first: seismic monitors picking up faint tremors, atmospheric sensors registering inexplicable temperature fluctuations. Sarah worked tirelessly to make sense of the data, her station in the lab becoming a shrine to spreadsheets and graphs. But the more she uncovered, the less sense any of it made.

"None of this adds up," she muttered one evening, her voice tight with frustration. She was hunched over her laptop, eyes bloodshot from too many hours staring at the screen. "What do you mean?" I asked, handing her a mug of coffee. "These readings—they're all over the place." She gestured to the screen, where rows of data scrolled endlessly. "We're seeing temperature spikes where there shouldn't be any, electromagnetic pulses with no apparent source... it's like the ice is alive." "Alive?" I repeated, raising an eyebrow. She sighed, leaning back in her chair. "Not literally. But something is happening out there, Larry. Something we don't understand."

The following day, the anomalies escalated. During a routine expedition to recalibrate one of the seismic sensors, Tom and I stumbled across a stretch of ice that was warmer to the touch. Not just warmer than the surrounding area—warm. "This doesn't make any sense," Tom said, kneeling to inspect the ice. His gloved hand hovered just above the surface, where a thin mist was rising. "Could it be geothermal activity?" I suggested, though even as I said it, I knew it didn't feel right. Tom shook his head. "Not here. We're nowhere near any volcanic hotspots. This shouldn't be possible." We took samples, documenting everything with photos and video. But as we worked, the unease grew stronger, gnawing at the edges of my mind. And it felt as though we were being watched, though I saw no one.

Back at the station, Sarah and Harrison examined the samples, their faces growing more concerned with each passing minute. "This composition..." Sarah said, trailing off as she stared at the microscope. "What is it?" I asked, leaning over her shoulder. "It's... different," she said finally. "The crystalline structure is unlike any ice I've ever seen. It's denser, almost... metallic." "Metallic ice?" Tom said, his tone incredulous. Harrison frowned, his expression unreadable. "We need to keep this quiet," he said, his voice low. "Until we know what we're dealing with, this stays between us."

That night, the whispers began. I was laying in my bunk, staring at the ceiling, when I heard it—a faint, almost imperceptible murmur. At first, I thought it was the wind, but the sound was too deliberate, too structured. It came in waves, rising and falling like a language I couldn't understand. I sat up, my heart pounding. The room was dark, save for the faint glow of the emergency lights. Everyone else was asleep, their breathing soft and even. But the whispers continued, growing louder, more insistent. I crept to the window, peering out into the frozen expanse. The landscape was bathed in pale moonlight, silent and still. But as I stared, I thought I saw something—a flicker of movement in the distance, just beyond the perimeter of the station. A shadow. I blinked, and it was gone.

The next morning, I told Sarah about the whispers. "You're not the only one," she said grimly. "Tom mentioned hearing something too. And one of the engineers swears he saw lights out on the ice last night." "Lights?" She nodded. "Bright, blue-green lights. Like the ones we saw in the fissures." I felt a chill run down my spine. "Do you think it's connected?" "I don't know," she admitted. "But I think we need to find out."

So over the next few days, the phenomena intensified. Equipment malfunctioned inexplicably, tools vanished only to reappear in strange places, and the whispers became almost constant. And at times, they seemed to be coming from inside the station itself, as though the very walls were conspiring against us. Harrison tried to keep everyone focused, but the cracks were beginning to show. Arguments broke out over trivial matters, tempers flared, and the sense of camaraderie that had defined our team began to crumble. "We need answers," Sarah said one evening, her voice shaking with frustration. "We can't keep pretending this is normal." "And what do you suggest?" Harrison snapped, his patience clearly wearing thin. "We can't exactly call for backup and explain we're hearing voices in the ice." "Then we figure it out ourselves," she said firmly. "We owe it to ourselves—and to science." Harrison sighed, rubbing his temples. "Fine. But we proceed with caution. Whatever this is, it's not something we want to provoke." As the week drew to a close, I found myself standing outside the station, staring at the horizon. The air was impossibly cold, biting at my exposed skin, but I didn't care. Something was out there—I could feel it. The ice hummed beneath my boots, a low, resonant vibration that seemed almost... expectant. And in the distance, I thought I saw them again—the faint, flickering lights. Whatever lay beneath the ice, it was waking up. And it was waiting for us.

(The Glimmer Beyond)

The next day began under an ominous sky, thick clouds swirling overhead like a warning written in gray. A sharp wind howled across the ice, rattling the station's steel supports and making every step outside feel like a battle. I zipped up my pack, pulling my hood tight as the team assembled for the morning briefing. Harrison's mood mirrored the weather. He stood at the front of the room, arms crossed, his sharp eyes scanning each of us. "Today's priority is an area southeast of the fissures," he announced. "Satellite imaging picked up anomalous thermal signatures—something we can't ignore." "Another anomaly?" Tom muttered under his breath. Harrison ignored him. "Sarah, Larry, you're with me. Tom, you and Miguel will stay here and continue monitoring the equipment. The rest of you, maintain the station." Sarah shot me a look as we prepared our gear. She didn't need to say anything; the apprehension in her eyes said it all.

Then moments later the journey was grueling. The wind fought us every step of the way, tearing at our jackets and whipping up snow until the landscape was nothing but a blinding white blur. Harrison led the way, his movements precise and deliberate. I followed close behind, with Sarah bringing up the rear. "Do you think this is connected to the fissures?" I called over the wind. "Too soon to tell," Harrison replied without turning around. Sarah caught up to me, her cheeks flushed from the cold. "It's more than connected," she said quietly. "It's all part of something bigger. I can feel it." I didn't argue. I felt it too.

The site was unremarkable at first glance—a flat expanse of ice stretching endlessly in all directions. But as we approached the coordinates, the air seemed to change. It was subtle, almost imperceptible, but I felt it—a shift in pressure, a faint vibration under my boots. Harrison stopped abruptly, raising a hand. "We're here." Sarah and I set to work, unpacking the equipment while Harrison marked the area. As I adjusted the thermal scanner, a strange sensation washed over me. It was as if the ground beneath us wasn't solid ice but something else entirely—something alive. "Getting anything?" Harrison asked, his voice breaking the silence. I checked the scanner, my heart skipping a beat. "There's... something." The screen displayed a faint heat signature, irregular and pulsating. It wasn't natural, that much was clear. Sarah peered over my shoulder. "It's moving." Harrison frowned. "Moving where?" "Up," I yelled.

Then the ice cracked. It was a sharp, deafening sound, like a gunshot echoing across the tundra. I stumbled backward, my heart pounding as a thin fissure snaked across the ground in front of me. "Back up!" Harrison shouted, grabbing my arm. We retreated several paces as the fissure widened, revealing a narrow crevice that seemed to glow faintly from within. The light was faint at first, barely noticeable against the white glare of the snow. But as we watched, it grew brighter, shifting through hues of blue, green, and gold. "What the hell is that?" Sarah whispered. Harrison didn't answer. He was staring into the crevice, his expression unreadable. I couldn't look away. The light was mesmerizing, its colors flowing like liquid, defying explanation. It felt... intelligent. "Sarah, take a sample," Harrison said finally, his voice tight. She hesitated, then knelt by the edge of the fissure, carefully lowering a small vial into the glowing ice. As she worked, I felt the vibration again—stronger this time, almost like a heartbeat. "Do you hear that?" I asked, my voice shaking. Sarah looked up, her face pale. "It's not just a sound," she said. "It's... speaking."

The whispers returned, louder than ever. They were indistinct, a blend of tones and cadences that made no sense yet felt hauntingly familiar. My pulse quickened as I strained to make out the words, but they slipped through my mind like water through fingers. Harrison's radio crackled, breaking the spell. "Base to Team One. Are you receiving?" He grabbed the radio. "This is Harrison. Go ahead." "Sir, we're picking up unusual readings on the seismic monitors. Is everything okay?" Harrison glanced at the fissure, then back at us. "We've encountered an anomaly," he said carefully. "We're collecting data now. Stand by." The light grew brighter, pulsating in time with the vibrations. I felt a strange pull, as though the fissure was calling to me. "Larry," Sarah said, her voice cutting through the haze. "Step back." I realized I had been inching closer to the edge, my hand outstretched toward the light. "Sorry," I muttered, shaking my head. "We've got what we need," Harrison said. "Let's move."

The trek back to the station felt longer than usual. The wind had died down, leaving an eerie silence in its wake. None of us spoke, each lost in our thoughts. When we finally reached the station, the others were waiting for us, their faces etched with concern. "What did you find?" Tom asked. Harrison didn't answer immediately. Instead, he handed the sample vial to Sarah. "Analyze this," he said. "I want results by morning."
"What about the light?" I asked. Harrison's eyes met mine, his expression unreadable. "We focus on the data," he said. "Everything else is secondary." That night, as I lay in my bunk, I couldn't stop thinking about the fissure. The light, the vibrations, the whispers—it was all connected. And deep down, I knew this was only the beginning. The glimmer beyond the ice wasn't just an anomaly. It was a message.

The next day I noticed that the air was sharper that morning, biting at the exposed edges of my face as we set out across the endless expanse. The sun hung low in the sky, casting long, cold shadows over the ice. There was a tension in the group, a shared anticipation that none of us wanted to voice. Harrison had barely spoken since our encounter with the glowing fissure the day before, but his movements were brisk, purposeful. "Stay close," he ordered, his breath visible in the freezing air. "We're heading toward the southern ridge." None of us questioned him. The fissures, the lights, the whispers—everything pointed southward, as if something beneath the ice was drawing us closer. The trek was arduous, the terrain growing steeper and more jagged as we approached the ridge. My legs ached from the climb, my breath coming in sharp, shallow bursts. But as we crested the ridge, all exhaustion fell away, replaced by sheer, uncomprehending awe. Then it happened below us, nestled within the ice, we saw a city.

At first glance, it looked like a mirage—an impossible vision shimmering against the stark white backdrop of the ice. But as I blinked and refocused, the details sharpened. Towering spires reached toward the sky, their surfaces smooth and glistening like polished glass. Domes and arches connected the structures, their curves impossibly elegant, defying any architectural style I'd ever seen. "Is this… real?" Sarah whispered. "It has to be," Tom replied, his tone wavering between awe and disbelief. Harrison didn't say anything. He simply stood there, his expression unreadable as his eyes scanned the city below. We descended cautiously, the air growing warmer as we approached the base of the ridge. The ice underfoot became smoother, almost like marble, reflecting the faint light of the overcast sky. By the time we reached the city's edge, the cold that had defined our every waking moment on the ice seemed to fade, replaced by a strange, almost pleasant warmth.

The structures towered over us, their surfaces etched with intricate patterns that seemed to shift and flow as I looked at them. It wasn't just a city—it was a masterpiece, a monument to something far beyond human comprehension. I reached out to touch one of the walls, half expecting it to vanish under my fingers. But it was solid, its surface cool and impossibly smooth. The patterns felt alive, pulsating faintly beneath my fingertips. "Who could have built this?" Sarah asked, her voice trembling with wonder. "No one we know," Harrison replied. We moved deeper into the city, our footsteps echoing eerily in the silence. There were no signs of life—no people, no animals, not even plants. And yet, the city didn't feel abandoned. It felt… waiting.

The streets were wide and paved with a material that glimmered faintly, like crushed gemstones. Each turn revealed new wonders: a plaza with a massive fountain frozen mid-spray, its water suspended in perfect crystalline arcs; a grand hall with pillars that seemed to hum faintly as we passed; and countless chambers filled with what looked like machines, their purposes as alien as their design. "This is impossible," Tom muttered, stopping to inspect one of the machines. "The technology—this is centuries, maybe millennia's, beyond anything we have." "And yet it's here," Sarah said, her eyes wide as she took in the room.

At the center of the city, we found what appeared to be a temple. It was the largest structure, its spire piercing the clouds above. The doors were massive, carved with symbols that seemed to shift and change when I looked directly at them. "Do we go in?" I asked, my voice barely above a whisper. Harrison nodded, his expression grim. "We didn't come all this way to turn back now." The doors swung open at the slightest touch, revealing an interior that defied logic. The walls were lined with panels that glowed faintly, illuminating a vast chamber filled with more of the strange machines. At the center of the room was a pedestal, its surface etched with the same shifting symbols as the doors. Sarah approached it cautiously, her fingers hovering over the symbols. "It's... warm," she said, glancing back at us. "Can you read it?" Harrison asked. She shook her head. "It's not any language I've seen. But it feels familiar, somehow."

We spent hours exploring the temple, documenting everything we could. But the more we discovered, the more questions arose. Why was the city empty? Who had built it? And what had happened to them? As the day wore on, a sense of unease began to creep in. The city was beautiful, breathtaking even, but it was also profoundly alien. Every structure, every artifact seemed to whisper of a purpose we couldn't comprehend. "This place wasn't meant for us," I said quietly as we regrouped outside the temple. Harrison nodded, his expression grim. "No, it wasn't. But now that we've found it, we need to understand it."

So as we prepared to head back to the station, I took one last look at the city. The setting sun cast long shadows over the spires, their surfaces catching the light and refracting it into a kaleidoscope of colors. It was beautiful, yes, but it was also a warning. Whatever had built this place, whatever had lived here, it wasn't gone. Not entirely. And as we turned to leave, I couldn't shake the feeling that we were being watched.

(The Guardians of the Ice)

Later that day I noticed that the stillness of the city broke as we prepared to leave. At first, it was faint—a low hum that vibrated through the air, barely perceptible. I stopped in my tracks, turning back toward the towering spires of the alien city. "Did anyone else hear that?" I asked, my voice echoing against the smooth walls of the temple.

Sarah froze mid-step, her eyes scanning the horizon. "It's not just a sound," she whispered. "It's... something alive."

Tom frowned, his hand hovering near the strap of his pack as though instinctively reaching for a weapon. "Alive? There's no one here, Sarah. It's just—" The hum grew louder, cutting him off. It wasn't mechanical. It wasn't natural, either. It was something deeper, something that resonated in the pit of my chest like a second heartbeat.

Harrison stepped forward, his expression more focused than alarmed. "Stay calm. Everyone stay together," he ordered. "We've stirred something, but we don't know what."

The source of the sound wasn't immediately clear, but its rhythm became unmistakable—a deliberate, intentional pattern, as if calling out to us. The city responded in kind, its glowing panels pulsing faintly, creating a light show that illuminated the twilight. "What is this?" Sarah asked, clutching her scanner as if it could provide answers. Harrison didn't reply. Instead, he raised a hand, signaling us to stay silent. The air grew warmer, almost stifling, and I noticed a faint mist creeping along the ground, rolling out from between the buildings.

Then it happened, the figures appeared.

At first, they were just shadows, barely distinguishable from the mist. But as they moved closer, they took form. Human form. There were three of them, their silhouettes tall and imposing, draped in flowing garments that shimmered like the city itself. Their faces were obscured by smooth, featureless masks that reflected the pale light, giving them an otherworldly presence. We froze. My breath caught in my throat as the figures stopped a few paces from us, their heads tilting slightly as if observing us. "Are they... human?" Tom asked, his voice trembling.

"They look human," Sarah whispered, "but that doesn't mean they are." One of the figures stepped forward, lifting a hand in what seemed to be a gesture of peace. "Who are you?" Harrison asked, his voice steady despite the tension crackling in the air. For a moment, there was no reply. Then, a voice echoed in my mind—not through the air, but directly into my thoughts. "We are the Guardians," it said. The tone was neither male nor female, young nor old. It simply *was.*

I glanced at the others, realizing from their wide eyes that they were hearing the same voice. "The Guardians of what?" Harrison asked aloud. "Of this place. Of this world," the voice replied. The figure lowered its hand, and the mask dissolved like mist, revealing a face that took my breath away. It was human—strikingly so—but there was something otherworldly about the perfection of their features, the luminous quality of their skin, and the piercing clarity of their eyes. "You're not from here," I said, the words escaping me before I could think. The Guardian turned its gaze to me, and I felt the weight of centuries in those eyes. "No. We came to this world long ago, seeking refuge." "Refuge from what?" Sarah asked. The Guardian hesitated, its expression unreadable. "From a dying star. From the destruction of the world that birthed us." I felt a shiver run down my spine. These weren't just humans—they were *humans from another planet.*

The Guardian gestured for us to follow, and despite our unease, we obeyed. They led us through the city, past towering structures that pulsed faintly with light. As we walked, the mist parted, revealing more Guardians emerging from the shadows. They moved silently, their steps graceful, their expressions unreadable. "They're watching us," Tom muttered under his breath. "They're assessing us," Sarah corrected, her gaze darting from one Guardian to the next. The lead Guardian stopped before a grand archway, its surface etched with the same shifting patterns we'd seen throughout the city. Beyond it was a chamber unlike anything we'd encountered—a vast, circular hall filled with swirling light and intricate machinery. "This is the heart of the city," the Guardian said. "The place where all knowledge is kept." The Guardian gestured toward a massive console at the center of the room. "This city was our sanctuary, a place to preserve our history, our culture, and our people. But it was also a prison."
"Prison?" I repeated, frowning. The Guardian's gaze turned somber. "When we arrived on this world, we sought to integrate with its native life. But our presence disrupted the balance. To protect both ourselves and the planet, we isolated ourselves here, hidden beneath the ice." "For how long?" Sarah asked, her voice tinged with disbelief.
"At least a Millennia," the Guardian replied.

I couldn't wrap my mind around it—an ancient human civilization, more advanced than anything we'd ever imagined, hidden beneath the ice for thousands of years. And yet, there they were, standing before us. "What do you want from us?" Harrison asked, his tone cautious. The Guardian tilted its head slightly, as if considering the question. "We want nothing. But you have disturbed our sanctuary, and now, the balance has been broken. What happens next depends on your choices." "Balance?" I asked. "What kind of balance?" The Guardian's expression darkened. "There are forces at work beyond this city, beyond even this planet. Forces that will not tolerate the disruption you have caused." The words hung in the air, heavy with implication.

As the Guardians led us back toward the edge of the city, I couldn't shake the feeling that we'd crossed a line—that our discovery of this place was more than just a scientific breakthrough. It was the beginning of something much larger, something we couldn't yet understand. "We will speak again," the lead Guardian said as we prepared to leave. "Wait," I said, turning back. "Why now? Why reveal yourselves to us?" The Guardian's eyes met mine, and for a moment, I thought I saw a flicker of something—fear, perhaps, or sorrow. "Because the time has come," it said. And then they were gone, their forms dissolving into the mist as if they'd never been there at all. We returned to the station in silence, each of us lost in our thoughts. The city, the Guardians, their warnings—it was too much to process. But one thing was clear. The ice wasn't just hiding a city. It was hiding a truth that could change everything.

A week had passed since we first met the Guardians of the ice, yet the encounter lingered in my mind as vividly as if it had just happened. The city, with its shimmering spires and shifting light, had become an obsession for all of us. It wasn't just the scientific implications that weighed on us; it was the realization that we weren't alone—that humans from another world had walked this Earth long before us. Each night, I found myself lying awake, replaying every moment of that first meeting, every word they spoke. But the Guardians had disappeared just as mysteriously as they had appeared, leaving us with more questions than answers. We'd spent the week mapping the city as much as possible, documenting the artifacts and technology within its boundaries. But the Guardians had made no further contact, and a strange unease settled over the group. The silence felt intentional, as if they were watching us, waiting for something.

That morning, as the sun rose weakly over the icy expanse, the hum returned. "Do you hear that?" Sarah asked, her voice cutting through the quiet. We were inside one of the smaller domed buildings near the city's edge, cataloging what looked like a storage facility. I froze mid-step, straining to listen. The sound was faint but unmistakable—a low, resonant vibration that seemed to come from everywhere and nowhere at once. "It's them," I said, my heart pounding. Harrison entered the room, his expression grim. "Gather your gear. We're going back to the central plaza." No one questioned him. Then we moved quickly, our movements automatic after days of exploration. The hum grew louder as we approached the heart of the city, where the massive temple loomed like a sentinel against the pale sky. When we reached the plaza, the mist was already gathering. It rolled across the ground like a living thing, swirling and coiling around the base of the temple.

The air was warmer here, almost stifling, and the light took on a strange, golden hue. "They're here," Tom said, his voice a mix of awe and fear.

The Guardians emerged from the mist as they had before, their movements fluid and deliberate. There were more of them this time—at least a dozen—each dressed in the same flowing garments that seemed to shimmer with an inner light. Their masks were back, reflecting the faint glow of the city. The lead Guardian stepped forward, its movements almost human but just uncanny enough to remind us of what they truly were. The mask dissolved, revealing the same luminous face I remembered. "Welcome back," the Guardian said, its voice echoing in my mind.

"Why now?" Harrison asked, his tone carefully measured. "Why return after a week of silence?" "We have observed you," the Guardian replied. "Your actions, your intentions. And we have determined that you may proceed." "Proceed with what?" Sarah asked, her voice tinged with both curiosity and caution. The Guardian gestured toward the temple. "With understanding. There is much you must know if you are to survive what is to come."

We followed the Guardians into the temple, moving deeper than we had during our initial exploration. The halls were lit by the same glowing panels, but the air felt different now—charged with an energy I couldn't quite describe. The Guardians led us to a massive chamber lined with what looked like screens or windows. As we entered, the panels flickered to life, displaying images that defied comprehension. One screen showed a planet—lush, green, and vibrant, with sprawling cities and towering structures that put even the greatest human achievements to shame. Another displayed a star, its surface roiling with violent flares. "This was our home," the Guardian said, its voice tinged with a sadness that I felt deep in my chest. "What happened to it?" I asked, unable to tear my eyes away from the images. The screen shifted, showing the planet again, but this time it was different. The skies were darkened, the land scorched, and the cities reduced to ruins. The star in the background burned brighter, its light consuming everything in its path. "Our sun was dying," the Guardian explained. "Its death destroyed our world. We had no choice but to flee." "And you came here?" Sarah asked. "We had little time to choose," the Guardian replied. "But this world was young, and its ecosystems fragile but adaptable. We made it our sanctuary." As the images faded, the Guardians turned to face us. "We integrated with this planet as best as we could," the lead Guardian continued. "But our presence was not without consequence. The balance of life was disrupted. To preserve the planet, we chose isolation." "Until now," Harrison said, his tone cautious.

The Guardian inclined its head. "Until now. The forces that drove us from our home are not confined to a single star system. They are ancient, relentless, and they are coming." My stomach twisted at the words. "Coming here?" I asked. "Yes," the Guardian said. "Your discovery of this city has accelerated the timeline. The balance is breaking, and the adversary will soon take notice." "Adversary?" Sarah repeated. The Guardian didn't elaborate, but the weight of the word hung heavily in the air. So we spent hours in the chamber, absorbing as much as we could. The Guardians explained their history in fragments, revealing glimpses of a civilization so advanced it bordered on the divine. They spoke of their journey across the stars, their integration with Earth, and the countless sacrifices they'd made to preserve the planet's fragile ecosystems. But they also spoke of the adversary—a force they described as ancient and unstoppable, one that had already consumed countless worlds. "Why tell us this now?" I asked. "What can we possibly do against something like that?" The Guardian's gaze bore into mine, its luminous eyes filled with an intensity that made my heart race. "Because you must. Your species has the potential to survive, to evolve beyond this crisis. But only if you choose to act."

Then by the time we left the temple, the sky was dark, and the mist had receded. The city seemed quieter now, as if it was waiting for us to make our next move. "Do you believe them?" Sarah asked as we trudged back to the station. Harrison didn't answer immediately. When he did, his voice was heavy. "I don't think it matters what we believe. This is bigger than us. Bigger than anything we've ever faced." I glanced back at the city, its spires glowing faintly in the distance. The Guardians had given us knowledge, but they'd also given us a burden—a responsibility we weren't ready for. And as we walked into the cold, unrelenting night, I couldn't shake the feeling that the adversary was already watching.

(Secrets of the Hidden City)

The next day, the Guardians called us back to the temple. It wasn't a request—they didn't speak in terms of asking or demanding. The hum that filled the air seemed to resonate in our very bones, pulling us toward the city's heart like a magnet. I hadn't slept much the night before. Every time I closed my eyes, I saw the Guardians' luminous faces and the terrifying images they'd shown us: a dying planet, a collapsing ecosystem, and a warning that echoed louder than any words. Now, as we approached the towering structure, I could feel the weight of something monumental about to unfold. "This feels different," Sarah murmured as we stepped through the archway into the temple.

Harrison nodded, his jaw tight. "They've been holding back. I think today, we're going to find out why."

Then I noticed that inside, the temple's grand chamber it was alive with light. The intricate patterns on the walls pulsed in sync with the Guardians' movements, and the air itself seemed to hum with energy. The lead Guardian, the one who had spoken to us before, stood at the center of the room, its robes shimmering like liquid silver. "Come," it said, its voice filling my mind. "The time has come to reveal what you seek." We gathered in a semi-circle around the Guardian, our breath visible in the chilly air. The other Guardians remained silent, their masked faces turned toward us like silent sentinels. "This city," the lead Guardian began, gesturing to the glowing walls around us, "is the last remnant of a civilization that once spanned the stars. It was not built here, on this planet. It was brought here, piece by piece, to serve as our sanctuary." "Brought here?" Tom asked, his voice filled with skepticism. "How is that even possible?" The Guardian turned its gaze to him, unblinking. "We harnessed energies your kind has yet to comprehend. To us, the fabric of space and time is as malleable as clay. This city was a vessel, a fortress, and a beacon. It carried us across the void to this world."

I exchanged a glance with Sarah, who was furiously scribbling notes in her journal. It was impossible to process. The city wasn't just ancient—it was alien in every sense of the word, a relic from a time and place we couldn't even fathom. "Why here?" I asked. "Why Earth?" The Guardian's expression softened, if such a thing was possible. "Earth was young and full of life. Its potential was unmatched among the worlds we discovered. We chose it not for its resources, but for its promise—a promise that your kind now carries forward." The Guardian moved to the center console, its hand hovering over the glowing surface. The lights shifted, forming a holographic display that filled the chamber. It showed a sprawling cityscape, far larger than the one we stood in, teeming with life.

"This was our home," the Guardian said, its voice tinged with sorrow. "A world of harmony and abundance, sustained by our knowledge and unity." The image shifted, showing massive towers emitting beams of energy into the sky. "But even we were not immune to hubris. We drew too deeply from our star, believing it would sustain us forever. In doing so, we sealed our fate." The hologram darkened, showing the same city in ruins, its towers crumbling as fire rained from the sky. The Guardians stood silent, their heads bowed.

"What happened to the others?" Harrison asked, breaking the heavy silence. "Many perished," the Guardian replied. "Others scattered across the cosmos, seeking refuge on distant worlds. We were among the fortunate few to find a haven." The hologram shifted again, this time showing Earth as it might have looked a millennia ago—a wild, untamed landscape teeming with life. The city descended from the sky, its glowing spires piercing the clouds as it settled into the icy expanse. "We integrated with the life forms here," the Guardian continued. "We shared knowledge, guided their development, and learned from them in turn. But as the ages passed, we saw the consequences of our presence. The balance of this world was fragile, and we were disrupting it."

"So you hid," Sarah said, piecing it together. "Yes," the Guardian said. "We buried the city beneath the ice, erasing our traces as much as possible. Then we became the Guardians—not of the city, but of this planet's future."

"What about now?" I asked, my voice trembling slightly. "Why come out of hiding after all this time?"

The Guardian's luminous eyes met mine, and I felt a chill that had nothing to do with the cold. "Because your species has reached a turning point. Your discoveries, your technologies, your ambitions—they echo the same paths we once walked. And like us, you face a choice: to preserve the balance, or to destroy it." It gestured to the glowing panels on the walls, which now displayed images of modern Earth—cities bustling with life, forests shrinking under the weight of human expansion, oceans choked with plastic. "This is your legacy," the Guardian said. "And it will determine the fate of not only your world but all who come after."

The room fell silent. I could feel the weight of their words pressing down on me, on all of us. The Guardians weren't just sharing their history—they were warning us, showing us a mirror of our own potential future.

"What can we do?" Harrison asked, his voice steady but strained. The Guardian stepped closer, its gaze unwavering. "Learn. Understand. And when the time comes, act. The adversary approaches, and it will test the strength of your kind. If you fail, this world will fall as ours did." The holograms faded, leaving the chamber in darkness save for the faint glow of the walls. The Guardians stood silently, their presence as commanding as ever. "Why us?" I asked. "Why show this to us?" The Guardian's expression softened again, almost imperceptibly. "Because you found us. And because you still have a choice."

We left the temple in silence, the weight of the Guardians' words heavy in our minds. The city felt different now—less like a relic and more like a living testament to what was at stake. As we walked back to the station, I couldn't shake the feeling that the Guardians' story wasn't just a warning. It was a challenge. And whether we were ready or not, the future of our world—and perhaps the entire galaxy—was in our hands.

Then a week had passed since the Guardians unveiled the origins of the hidden city and their tragic history. And the weight of their revelations had settled over our team like a fog, thick and unshakable. Yet, despite the enormity of their story, it seemed they had more to tell. The invitation came as it always did, through the hum in the air. This time, it resonated even deeper, pulling at something primal within me. It wasn't a call we could resist; it was as if the city itself demanded our presence. "I don't think they're done with us," Harrison muttered as we gathered our equipment. "They're peeling back the layers," Sarah said, her expression a mixture of awe and trepidation. "One piece at a time." I adjusted my pack and glanced toward the temple. Its towering silhouette seemed more imposing than ever, as if it were growing in stature with every revelation. "Let's find out what's behind the next layer," I said, more to myself than to anyone else.

The Guardians were waiting for us inside the grand chamber, their forms bathed in the soft, shifting light of the walls. This time, there were no holograms, no immediate displays of their advanced technology. Instead, the atmosphere was heavier, the air charged with an intensity that made the hairs on the back of my neck stand up.

The lead Guardian stepped forward, its luminous eyes meeting each of ours in turn. "You have accepted the burden of knowledge," it said. "But there is more you must understand." "We're listening," Harrison replied, his voice steady. The Guardian inclined its head slightly, a gesture that might have been approval. "This city is not merely a relic of our past. It is a key—a nexus of energy and knowledge, connected to the fabric of the universe itself. Its presence here was not an accident."

The walls began to shimmer, their light coalescing into patterns and shapes. Unlike the holograms from before, these images were abstract, shifting geometries that seemed to pulse with a life of their own.

"When we chose this planet as our refuge," the Guardian continued, "we did so with the understanding that it held unique properties—an alignment of forces that made it unlike any other world we had encountered." "What kind of forces?" Sarah asked, her pen poised above her notebook. "Energetic ley lines," the

Guardian replied, its voice resonating with a strange harmony. "Paths of power that crisscross the planet, converging here, beneath the ice. This city was built to harness those energies, to stabilize and amplify them."

The shimmering patterns shifted again, forming a map of Earth. Thin, glowing lines traced intricate pathways across the globe, converging in several key locations. One of the brightest points was directly beneath the city. "This is why we chose this location," the Guardian said. "It is a focal point, a place where the energies of the Earth and the cosmos align. The city was designed not only to sustain us but to protect this balance."

"What happens if the balance is broken?" I asked, the question escaping before I could stop it. The Guardian's gaze fixed on me, its intensity almost overwhelming. "Destruction," it said simply. "Not just of this city, but of the planet itself. These energies are both a gift and a responsibility. Misuse them, and the consequences are catastrophic."

A new image appeared, this one showing the city as it might have looked in its prime. The spires glowed with an inner light, their tips connected by arcs of energy that crackled like lightning. At the center of it all was the temple, its structure radiating waves of power that spread outward like ripples in a pond. "This is the city at its full potential," the Guardian explained. "A living organism, attuned to the rhythms of the planet and the stars. But such power requires balance, and balance requires understanding." "So why tell us this now?" Harrison asked, his voice edged with suspicion. "What are we supposed to do with this knowledge?" The Guardian paused, its luminous eyes dimming slightly. "Because the adversary you face will seek to disrupt this balance. They will attempt to harness the city's power for their own ends, and in doing so, they will bring about its destruction." The room fell silent as we absorbed the implications of the Guardian's words. It wasn't just a warning; it was a call to action. "What kind of adversary are we talking about?" Sarah asked. "You've mentioned them before, but we need specifics." The Guardian hesitated, as if choosing its words carefully. "They are remnants of a great conflict, beings who seek to consume and control. They are not bound by the limitations of your kind. They will come in many forms, some familiar, others incomprehensible. And they will stop at nothing to claim what lies here." I swallowed hard, my throat suddenly dry. "You're saying they're already coming?" The Guardian's gaze shifted toward me, and I felt the weight of its answer before it even spoke. "Yes. The city's reawakening has drawn their attention. The time is short."

The shifting patterns on the walls grew brighter, their movements more erratic. The air buzzed with energy, and I felt a strange sensation in my chest, as if my heartbeat were syncing with the pulsing light. "What is this?" Tom asked, his voice rising with alarm. "It is the city's resonance," the Guardian replied. "It is responding to your presence, attuning itself to your frequencies. This connection is vital. Without it, you cannot hope to protect what lies here." "What do you mean by 'protect'?" I asked. The Guardian stepped closer, its towering form casting a long shadow. "You are the inheritors of this knowledge, the stewards of this place. Whether you accept this role or not, the responsibility is now yours."

We left the temple hours later, our minds reeling from the weight of what we had learned. The Guardians had given us more than just the secrets of the city—they had given us a mission. As we trudged back to the station, I couldn't shake the feeling that we were standing on the edge of something far greater than ourselves. The Guardians had entrusted us with their legacy, but they had also made it clear that the stakes were higher than we could imagine.

And as the icy winds whipped around us, I knew one thing for certain: there was no turning back.

(Wonders of Another World)

As we continued to Explore the Ice City felt like stepping into the pages of a science fiction novel. Every corridor, every chamber, every faint hum of energy spoke of a civilization so far beyond anything we'd ever known that it almost felt like magic. Yet, as I walked through its gleaming halls, I realized how grounded it all was. The Guardians' technology wasn't designed to dazzle; it was designed to function in harmony with the world around it. So we began our exploration the day after the Guardians shared more of the city's origins. The Guardians had given us free rein to wander certain parts of the city, though they warned us not to venture into restricted zones. They didn't elaborate on what we might find if we ignored their warnings, and none of us were eager to find out.

Our first stop was a chamber the Guardians referred to as the Nexus. It was a vast, circular room with a ceiling so high it disappeared into shadows. The walls were lined with what looked like crystalline panels, each one glowing softly with different colors. At the center of the room stood a column of light that stretched from floor to ceiling, pulsing with a rhythmic, almost hypnotic energy. "This is the city's heart," one of the Guardians explained, its voice resonating in my mind. "It regulates the flow of energy throughout the city, ensuring balance and stability." Sarah approached the column, her eyes wide with wonder. "Is it alive?" she asked. "In a sense," the Guardian replied. "It is a symbiotic system, both mechanical and organic. It adapts, evolves, and responds to the needs of the city and its inhabitants." I reached out, not to touch it, but to feel the energy radiating from it. A tingling sensation danced along my skin, and for a moment, I felt connected to something far greater than myself.

From the Nexus, we moved on to what the Guardians called the Hall of Records. This chamber was smaller, more intimate, but no less awe-inspiring. The walls were covered in what looked like holographic text and images, shifting and changing as we approached. "This is where our knowledge is stored," the Guardian explained. "Every discovery, every advancement, every lesson learned is preserved here." Sarah immediately began asking questions, her curiosity as boundless as ever. "Can we access it? Can we learn from it?" The Guardian tilted its head, considering her request. "You may observe, but you must tread carefully. Knowledge without understanding can be dangerous."

As I scanned the glowing walls, I saw glimpses of the Guardians' history— their home world, their exodus, and the construction of the Ice City. But there were other images, too, ones that sent chills down my spine: dark, shadowy figures, massive ships blotting out the stars, and planets consumed by fire. "These are the adversaries you spoke of?" I asked, my voice shaking slightly. "Yes," the Guardian said. "And they are closer than you realize."

The next chamber we visited was unlike anything I'd ever seen. The Guardians called it the Arboretum, but it was far more than a simple garden. Towering trees with glowing leaves stretched toward the ceiling, their roots entwined with the crystalline floor. Streams of water flowed in perfect harmony with the paths, their surfaces shimmering with iridescent colors. "It's beautiful," Sarah said, her voice filled with awe. "It's more than that," Harrison added, crouching to examine one of the streams. "This entire place is a closed ecosystem. It's self-sustaining." The Guardian nodded. "It is a microcosm of what your world could be. A balance between technology and nature, each enhancing the other." I walked through the Arboretum in silence, taking in the sights, sounds, and smells. It was a place of peace, of life, and yet, I couldn't shake the feeling that it was also a reminder—a vision of what Earth could become, or what it might lose.

Our exploration continued into the residential areas of the city, where the Guardians had once lived. The chambers were sparse but elegant, their designs emphasizing function over form. There were no personal belongings, no signs of individuality. It was clear that the Guardians valued the collective over the self. "This must have been a lonely existence," Tom said, running his hand along a smooth, featureless wall. The Guardian nearest to us responded, its voice tinged with something that might have been regret. "Loneliness is a construct of your species. For us, unity was our strength." I couldn't imagine living like that—without personal space, without individuality. But as I thought about it, I realized that the Guardians' way of life had allowed them to survive when so many others had perished. The most astonishing part of our journey came at the end of the day when we were allowed to visit the city's transportation hub. The room was massive, its walls lined with sleek, oblong vessels that hovered a few inches above the ground. "These were our ships," the Guardian explained. "They carried us across the stars, through the void, and eventually to this planet." Harrison stepped closer to one of the vessels, his hand hovering just above its surface. "They look untouched," he said. "They are dormant," the Guardian replied. "But they remain functional, should the need arise." "Could we—" Sarah began, but the Guardian cut her off. "No. These vessels are not for your use. Their power is beyond your understanding, and their purpose is not aligned with your species' path." So as the day drew to a close, we returned to the Nexus. The Guardians gathered around us, their luminous eyes reflecting the pulsing light of the city's heart. "You have seen much," the lead Guardian said. "But there is still more to learn. The city holds secrets even we do not fully comprehend. It is as much a mystery to us as it is to you." I looked around at my team, their faces a mix of wonder, fear, and determination. Because we had been given a glimpse into a world far beyond our own, a world of possibilities and dangers we could barely comprehend. And as I stood there, bathed in the city's light, I realized that our journey was only just beginning.

Another week had passed since our initial exploration of the hidden city beneath the ice. In that time, the Guardians had granted us more access to its advanced technologies and deeper insights into their way of life. The awe I'd felt during our first journey through the city hadn't faded—it had only grown more profound. The city felt alive, constantly revealing new wonders with each passing day. It was clear the Guardians were deliberate in their guidance. They revealed knowledge in layers, ensuring we absorbed the significance of one marvel before showing us another. Their methodical approach mirrored the city itself: precise, harmonious, and endlessly intricate.

Our second week of exploration began with a return to the Nexus. The crystalline panels now displayed intricate patterns and symbols that shifted as we moved. The Guardians explained these were representations of the city's energy flows, a living map of its power systems. "This is new," Sarah said, her voice tinged with excitement. "The city adapts," the lead Guardian replied. "It recognizes your presence and seeks to communicate." "Communicate how?" I asked, unable to tear my eyes from the swirling symbols. "Through resonance," the Guardian said. "Each of you emits a unique frequency. The city learns these frequencies and aligns itself to them, creating a shared understanding." I didn't entirely grasp the mechanics, but I felt the truth of its words. The energy in the room felt more attuned to us than before, as if the city were welcoming us deeper into its fold.

From the Nexus, we were led to a chamber the Guardians called the Atelier. This was their hub for innovation and creation, a place where ideas became reality. The room was vast, filled with structures that seemed to blur the line between machines and organic life. "What is all this?" Harrison asked, gesturing to a cluster of tendrils that pulsed with light. "These are fabricators," the Guardian explained. "They construct and deconstruct matter at the molecular level, allowing us to create anything we require." Sarah's eyes widened. "Anything? You're saying you could create food, tools, even buildings from scratch?" "Precisely," the Guardian replied. "It is a process of transformation, not unlike the cycles of your natural world." I watched as one of the fabricators came to life, its tendrils weaving together streams of light. In moments, the light solidified into a small, crystalline object. "It's like watching magic," Tom said, his voice barely above a whisper. "Magic is merely science you do not yet understand," the Guardian said, its tone almost amused.

Our next destination was the Observatory, a chamber that opened my eyes to the sheer scope of the Guardians' understanding. The walls were lined with what looked like translucent screens, displaying vivid images of stars, planets, and galaxies. "This is where we studied the cosmos," the Guardian said. "We sought to understand our place within the universe, much as your species does." Sarah was the first to approach one of the screens. As she touched it, the image shifted, zooming in on a nebula that shimmered with hues of violet and gold. "This is incredible," she said, her voice filled with wonder. "It's like having the universe at your fingertips." I moved to another screen, which displayed a glowing sphere surrounded by swirling rings. "What is this?" I asked. "A world we once called home," the Guardian replied, its voice tinged with a sadness that resonated in my chest. "It no longer exists, but its memory remains here."

Later in the week, the Guardians introduced us to another aspect of their way of life: their relationship with time. They led us to a chamber called the Chronos Vault, a place where time itself seemed to bend and flow in ways I couldn't comprehend. "This chamber allows us to observe and interact with different points in time," the Guardian explained. "How is that possible?" Harrison asked, his skepticism evident. "Time is not linear," the Guardian replied. "It is a fabric, woven with threads that can be traced and manipulated. Here, we can revisit our past and glimpse potential futures." I felt a chill run down my spine as the walls began to shimmer, displaying scenes from the Guardians' history. I saw another one of their exoduses, their struggles, and their triumphs. But then the images shifted, showing glimpses of Earth—our wars, our achievements, and something else: a shadowy figure standing in the ruins of a city. "Is that... a warning?" I asked. "Potential futures are not fixed," the Guardian said. "They are possibilities, shaped by the choices you make."

The week culminated with a visit to what the Guardians called the Sanctuary. This was the heart of their way of life, a place of reflection and unity. The chamber was filled with a soft, golden light that seemed to emanate from the air itself. "This is where we came to harmonize our energies," the Guardian explained. "To connect with each other and with the city." The air was thick with a sense of peace, a stillness that seemed to quiet even my racing thoughts. The Guardians invited us to sit in the center of the chamber, where the light was brightest. And as I sat down, I felt a warmth spread through my body, as if the city itself were embracing me. Then for a moment, I was aware of everything—the hum of the Nexus, the pulse of the Arboretum, the flow of energy through the city's veins. "This is what we sought to preserve," the Guardian said. "A balance, a unity that transcends the individual." But when we finally left the city that day, I couldn't help but feel changed. The Guardians had shown us wonders I never could have imagined, but they had also given us a glimpse of what humanity could aspire to. So as we walked back to the station, Harrison broke the silence. "Do you think we'll ever reach their level?" I didn't answer right away. Instead, I looked back at the city, its spires glowing softly in the distance. "Maybe," I said at last. "But only if we learn to see the world the way they do—not as something to conquer, but as something to protect."

(The Icy Wilderness)

As me and the team continued on our journey one of the Guardians announced they would take us beyond the city's protective walls to explore the icy wilderness, I felt a mix of excitement and apprehension. The Ice City had been a marvel, a testament to the capabilities of an advanced civilization, but stepping into the uncharted expanse outside its borders was something entirely different. We gathered in the Arboretum before our departure, the Guardians preparing us for what lay ahead. They provided us with cloaks lined with a thin, metallic fabric that adjusted to the temperature. The material was light and flexible, but as soon as I donned it, warmth spread through me like a second skin. "These will protect you from the elements," the lead Guardian said. "The wilderness is harsh and unforgiving, but it is also teeming with life—life unlike anything you have encountered before." I exchanged a glance with Sarah, who was already securing her gear. Harrison, ever the skeptic, muttered something about not trusting the Guardians' "futuristic blankets," but he slipped one on anyway.

    The journey out of the city began through a vast tunnel, its walls shimmering with faint blue light. The temperature dropped noticeably as we walked, but the cloaks did their job, insulating us against the cold. After what felt like hours, we emerged into a landscape that took my breath away. The icy wilderness stretched as far as the eye could see, a pristine expanse of snow and ice punctuated by jagged peaks and glittering formations. The sky above was a deep, crystalline blue, and the air was so clear it felt like my lungs were being cleansed with every breath. "This is incredible," Sarah said. "The ice is ancient," the Guardian said, its voice resonating in our minds. "It holds the history of this world and others." As we moved deeper into the wilderness, the Guardians began pointing out signs of life. At first, they were subtle: faint tracks in the snow, shadows flitting across the horizon. Then, we encountered our first true marvel.

    It was a creature unlike anything I'd ever seen—a large, quadrupedal animal with translucent fur that shimmered in the sunlight. Its eyes were a deep, iridescent green, and its movements were graceful, almost ethereal. "What is that?" Harrison asked, his voice filled with a rare note of awe. "A Glacivor," the Guardian replied. "It feeds on the minerals in the ice, extracting nutrients that sustain its unique biology." We watched as the creature lowered its massive head, its tongue—a glowing, bioluminescent appendage—lapping at the ice. The Guardians explained that its fur contained microscopic crystals that helped regulate its body temperature, allowing it to survive in the extreme cold.

Then as we continued, the terrain grew more challenging. The ice gave way to rocky outcroppings, and the wind picked up, howling like a living entity. It was then that we encountered another species, this one far more elusive. High above us, perched on a jagged cliff, was a birdlike creature with wings that seemed to be made of ice. Its feathers glistened in the sunlight, and when it took flight, it left a trail of shimmering particles in its wake. "A Cryophorus," the Guardian said. "It uses the particles from its wings to scatter light, confusing predators." "Predators?" Sarah asked, glancing around nervously. "They are rare in this region," the Guardian reassured us. "But they exist."

So as the day wore on, we came across a vast crevasse that seemed to pulse with light. Peering over the edge, I saw streams of luminescent liquid flowing through the ice, casting an otherworldly glow on the walls of the chasm. "This is a lifeline," the Guardian said. "The liquid contains microorganisms that form the foundation of the ecosystem here. They are the building blocks of the life you have encountered." Harrison knelt down, carefully collecting a sample of the glowing substance in a vial. "This could rewrite everything we know about extremophiles," he said, his earlier skepticism replaced by genuine fascination.

The final stop on our journey was a massive ice cave, its entrance marked by towering pillars of crystal that sparkled like diamonds. Inside, the air was warmer, and the walls were covered in bioluminescent moss that bathed the chamber in soft, green light. "This cave is a sanctuary," the Guardian explained. "Many species come here to rest and heal." As if on cue, a group of small, fox-like creatures emerged from the shadows. Their fur was a deep blue, and their eyes glowed softly in the dim light. They watched us with curiosity but showed no fear. "They are Frostlings," the Guardian said. "They are highly intelligent and have developed a symbiotic relationship with the cave's ecosystem." One of the Frostlings approached me, its head tilted inquisitively. I crouched down, extending a hand. To my surprise, it nuzzled against my palm, its fur cool to the touch but not unpleasantly so.

Then as we made our way back to the city, I couldn't help but feel a deep sense of humility. The wilderness we had explored was as much a part of the Guardians' legacy as the city itself. It was a reminder that life, in all its forms, could thrive even in the harshest conditions. "What do you think?" Sarah asked as we trudged through the snow. "I think we've only scratched the surface," I said, glancing back at the glowing cave in the distance. "There's so much more to learn—about them, about this place, and about ourselves." And as the city's spires came into view, their soft light piercing the twilight, I realized just how small we were in the grand tapestry of the universe. But for the first time, that didn't feel daunting. It felt inspiring.

And one week after our initial venture into the icy wilderness, the Guardians decided it was time to reveal more of this vast and enigmatic landscape. This time, we were promised a deeper dive—both literally and figuratively—into the mysteries that lay beyond the city's boundaries. The first excursion had left us in awe, but as we prepared for this second journey, I couldn't help but wonder: What else could possibly be out here? The journey began at dawn. The Guardians led us along a different path, this one descending into a series of ice tunnels that glowed faintly in the low light. The crystalline walls seemed to hum with energy, a soft, rhythmic pulse that matched the pace of our footsteps. "These tunnels were formed by the flows of ancient rivers," the lead Guardian explained. "They connect the surface to the deeper ecosystems below." "Deeper ecosystems?" Harrison asked, his tone a mix of curiosity and trepidation. The Guardian nodded. "You will see soon enough."

After what felt like hours of walking, the tunnel opened into a massive cavern, its ceiling so high it disappeared into darkness. The floor was covered in a thick, spongy moss that emitted a soft, golden glow. Scattered throughout the cavern were towering spires of ice, each one shimmering with hues of blue, green, and violet. "This is incredible," Sarah whispered. "It's like stepping into another world," I said, my breath fogging in the cold air.

Then as we ventured further into the cavern, the first of the new species revealed itself. It was a creature resembling a giant beetle, its shell covered in iridescent patterns that shifted as it moved. Its antennae glowed faintly, and it seemed to navigate the cavern with an almost otherworldly grace. "Lumicarapace," the Guardian said. "It plays a vital role in maintaining the balance of this ecosystem, consuming the moss and dispersing its spores." Then deeper into the cavern, we came across a subterranean lake, its surface so still it looked like glass. Beneath the water, luminous shapes darted back and forth, their movements casting ripples of light across the cavern walls. "What are those?" Sarah asked, kneeling at the water's edge. "They are Cryofins," the Guardian replied. "They thrive in these frigid waters, their bioluminescent patterns used for communication and navigation." Harrison crouched next to Sarah, his scientific instincts kicking in. "If we could study these, we might gain insights into how life can adapt to extreme conditions." I stood back, watching the glowing fish as they swirled in intricate, almost hypnotic patterns. It was hard not to feel a sense of wonder—and a little envy—at how perfectly they seemed to fit into their environment.

Then our next discovery was both startling and beautiful. As we made our way through a narrower section of the cavern, a sudden burst of movement caught my eye. A flock of small, bird-like creatures took to the air, their translucent wings catching the light and scattering it is like a prism. "Glacier Sparrows," the Guardian said as we watched them flit from one ice spire to

42

another. "They are highly social creatures, their wings designed to both camouflage and communicate." Then one of the sparrows landed on a nearby spire, its tiny body pulsating with light. It seemed to watch us, its head cocked inquisitively. "They're not afraid of us," I said, stepping closer. "They have no reason to be," the Guardian replied. "This ecosystem exists in harmony, free from the predatory hierarchies you are accustomed to."

The final discovery of the day took us to another cavern, this one smaller and warmer. The walls were covered in a thick layer of bioluminescent fungi, and the air was filled with a faint, earthy scent. At the center of the cavern was a creature that looked like a cross between a sloth and a bear, its fur a deep, midnight blue. "This is an Icebound Sentinel," the Guardian said. "A gentle giant that plays a critical role in maintaining the balance of the fungi and moss within this ecosystem." The Sentinel moved slowly, its massive paws carefully navigating the cavern floor. Despite its size, there was a grace to its movements, as if it were aware of every step it took. "It's beautiful," Sarah said, her voice tinged with awe. I nodded, unable to take my eyes off the creature. "It's like everything here was designed to fit perfectly together."

Then as we made our way back to the surface, I couldn't help but reflect on what we had seen. The icy wilderness was more than just a harsh, unyielding landscape—it was a living, breathing world, full of life forms that had adapted to its unique challenges. "What do you think?" Harrison asked as we emerged into the fading light of the surface. "I think there's so much we still don't understand," I said, glancing back at the tunnel entrance. "But that's what makes it so incredible." The Guardians had once again expanded our understanding of what was possible. And as we made our way back to the city, I couldn't help but feel a growing sense of responsibility—not just to learn from this world, but to protect it.

(Facing The Unknown)

The next day a announcement came early one morning, just as the icy sun was casting its faint light over the towering spires of the hidden city. The Guardians had deemed us ready for our first real expedition into the vast, mysterious expanse beyond the city. Unlike our guided tours of the past, this journey would test not just our endurance but our ability to survive in an environment unlike anything we'd ever faced. "This is not a journey for the faint of heart," the lead Guardian told us in the grand chamber. Its voice, as always, resonated with a calm authority. "The land beyond the city holds wonders and dangers in equal measure. Prepare well, for this is a path from which there may be no easy return." The weight of its words settled heavily on us. This wasn't just another exploration—it was a mission that could change everything.

Our preparations began in earnest. The Guardians provided us with equipment tailored to the conditions we would face, each piece imbued with the advanced technology they had perfected over centuries. The cloaks we had worn during our earlier excursions were replaced with full-bodied suits that regulated temperature, monitored vital signs, and provided a protective barrier against the elements. I held mine up to the light, marveling at its sleek design. "This looks like something out of a sci-fi movie," I said, running my fingers over the smooth, metallic fabric. "It's light, but it feels indestructible," Sarah added, already zipping hers up. Harrison was less enthusiastic. "Let's hope it holds up better than my old snow gear back home," he muttered, though even he couldn't hide his curiosity about the suit's intricate features.

The Guardians also introduced us to a series of tools and devices that would aid us on our journey. One of the most impressive was a multi-functional pack that could transform into a small shelter, a water purifier, or even a power source for other equipment. "This pack alone is a game-changer," Harrison said, examining its modular components. "With something like this, you could survive almost anywhere." "Let's hope it doesn't come to that," Sarah replied, her voice tinged with nervous laughter. Another notable device was a scanning instrument that the Guardians called the Luminar. It was capable of detecting life forms, analyzing geological samples, and even mapping the terrain in real time. When the Guardians demonstrated it, the holographic display lit up with a three-dimensional rendering of the surrounding area, complete with glowing markers indicating nearby life forms. "This is incredible," I said, my eyes glued to the display. "It's like having an entire research lab in your hands."

In addition to the equipment, the Guardians also provided us with sustenance specifically designed for the journey. The food came in compact, crystalline capsules that dissolved in water, releasing a nutrient-rich solution. While it wasn't exactly gourmet, it was surprisingly palatable and packed enough energy to sustain us through the most grueling conditions. "It's not bad," I said, swallowing a mouthful of the citrus-flavored solution. "Better than the MREs I had in the military," Harrison admitted, though his tone was still gruff. The Guardians even taught us how to forage for sustenance in the wilderness, identifying edible mosses and fungi that could supplement our supplies. They emphasized the importance of balance, warning us not to disrupt the fragile ecosystem.

So as we prepared our gear, the Guardians gave us a detailed briefing about the terrain we would encounter. They projected a holographic map of the surrounding area, highlighting key landmarks and potential hazards. "There are regions of unstable ice," the lead Guardian explained, pointing to a glowing red section of the map. "Avoid these at all costs. The depths beneath are treacherous and unforgiving." The Guardians also spoke of a mysterious phenomenon known as the Frost Veil, a shimmering barrier of ice and energy that stretched across parts of the wilderness. "What's beyond it?" Sarah asked, her voice filled with wonder. "That is for you to discover," the Guardian replied enigmatically.

The final stage of our preparation was physical training. While the Guardians couldn't replicate the exact conditions of the wilderness, they created a simulated environment that tested our endurance and adaptability. The training was grueling, but it gave us a glimpse of what we might face. By the end of each session, my muscles ached, and my breath came in ragged gasps, but I felt stronger, more prepared. Sarah, ever the optimist, kept pushing us with her relentless energy, while Harrison's gruff determination kept us grounded. "We're going to make it," Sarah said one evening as we sat in the simulation chamber, sweat dripping from our brows. "We've got each other, and we've got the Guardians. That's enough." I nodded, though a small part of me couldn't shake the nagging feeling that we were venturing into the unknown in more ways than one.

And the night before our departure, we gathered in the Arboretum for one last briefing. The Guardians stood before us, their ethereal forms glowing softly in the dim light. "Remember," the lead Guardian said, "this journey is not just about discovery. It is about understanding—of the land, of each other, and of yourselves. Trust in your instincts and in the bond you share as a team." As we left the chamber, I couldn't help but feel a mixture of excitement and trepidation. The weight of what lay ahead was daunting, but it was also exhilarating. For the first time in my life, I felt like I was on the cusp of something truly extraordinary. In the quiet moments before sleep, I went over my gear one last time, checking and rechecking each piece. My heart raced as I imagined what the next day would bring. "This is it," I whispered to myself. "The beginning of something bigger than any of us." The icy wilderness stretched before us, endless and unyielding, like a frozen ocean that had been still for a millennia. A week into our first real expedition, the team had begun to settle into a rhythm, though the challenges of this alien terrain tested us daily.

The Guardians had been right—this was no place for the faint of heart. Temperatures dipped so low that even the advanced suits they had provided struggled to keep us warm. The air itself felt heavy, dense with a stillness that seemed to amplify every sound we made. Even the smallest footstep on the snow echoed faintly, as if the land were whispering back at us. The landscape was a study in contradictions. Then one moment, we were traversing fields of ice so smooth and reflective they seemed like mirrors, our distorted reflections staring back at us. The next, we were navigating jagged ridges and deep crevasses, their sharp edges glinting like knives in the weak sunlight. Harrison, ever the pragmatist, led the way with the Luminar, its holographic map guiding us around the most treacherous areas. "Watch your step," he called back as we approached a narrow ice bridge spanning a deep chasm. "This thing doesn't look stable." "I don't think anything here is," Sarah muttered, clutching her pack tightly. I brought up the rear, my eyes scanning the horizon. There was something both mesmerizing and unsettling about the emptiness around us. It was beautiful, yes, but it was also unforgiving.

Despite the harsh conditions, the icy wilderness was not without its wonders. On our third day out, we stumbled upon a forest of ice spires, each one towering over us like a crystalline tree. The spires emitted a faint glow, their light shifting and pulsating in rhythm with the wind. "What do you think causes that?" Sarah asked, running her gloved hand along the surface of one spire. "Some kind of bioluminescence, maybe," Harrison replied, scanning the spire with the Luminar. "But it's like nothing I've ever seen before." The Guardians, who had accompanied us for this portion of the journey, offered little explanation. "The land speaks in its own way," one of them said cryptically. "Listen carefully, and you may learn its secrets."

Then on the fifth day, we encountered our first sign of life beyond the ice city. It came in the form of a herd of creatures resembling a cross between deer and wolves. Their fur was thick and silvery, blending seamlessly with the snowy landscape, and their eyes glowed faintly in the dim light. "Silverstalkers," the lead Guardian said, watching as the creatures moved gracefully across the ice. "They are both predators and prey, their survival a delicate balance within this ecosystem." Then one of the creatures paused, its gaze locking onto us. For a moment, the only sound was the soft crunch of snow beneath its feet. Then, with a flick of its tail, it bounded away, disappearing into the distance. "I feel like we're intruding," I said softly, watching the herd vanish. "In a way, we are," the Guardian replied. "But the land is patient. It has seen many come and go." By the seventh day, the strain of the journey was beginning to show. Our bodies ached from the constant exertion, and the cold gnawed at us despite our protective gear. But there was also a sense of camaraderie that had begun to form—a bond forged through shared struggle. That evening, as we set up camp on a plateau overlooking a vast ice plain, we gathered around the small energy field that served as our heat source. The Guardians had stepped away, giving us a rare moment of privacy. "Hard to believe it's only been a week," Sarah said, sipping from her water flask. "Feels like a lifetime," Harrison agreed, leaning back against his pack.

I stared out at the horizon, where the faint glow of the Frost Veil shimmered in the distance. "Whatever's out there," I said, "it's worth it. We've seen things no one else on Earth ever has." Sarah smiled, her exhaustion momentarily forgotten. "And we've only just begun." As the others settled in for the night, I stayed up a while longer, unable to shake the feeling that the land was watching us. The Guardians' words echoed in my mind: The land speaks in its own way. Listen carefully. I closed my eyes, letting the cold wind wash over me. In the distance, the faint howls of Silverstalkers echoed across the ice, a haunting melody that seemed to carry a message I couldn't quite understand. This was a place of mystery and wonder, of beauty and danger. And though it tested us at every turn, I knew I wouldn't trade this experience for anything.

(Through The Vail)

Later on as the team and I continued are journey the Frost Veil shimmered before us, a translucent curtain of energy and ice stretching as far as the eye could see. Its beauty was breathtaking, but there was an undeniable sense of trepidation in the air. For days, we had speculated about what lay beyond it—if the Guardians' cryptic warnings were anything to go by, this was a threshold few had ever crossed. "We're really doing this," Sarah whispered, her breath fogging up the frigid air. "We didn't come this far to turn back now," Harrison said, his voice steady but his eyes betraying a flicker of unease. As for me, I couldn't speak. My heart raced as we stepped closer to the Veil, its icy light casting strange shadows across our faces. The Guardians had told us it was safe to pass through, but their tone had held a gravity that suggested this was no small feat. "Stay close together," the lead Guardian instructed. "The Veil will challenge you, but it will not harm you if your intentions are pure." With a deep breath, I took the first step.

Passing through the Veil was unlike anything I'd ever experienced. It wasn't just a physical sensation—though the cold that bit into my skin felt sharper than anything I'd known—it was an emotional and mental journey, too. Flashes of memories, dreams, and fears flooded my mind, as if the Veil was peeling back layers of who I was. Then, just as suddenly as it began, it was over. I stumbled forward, my knees hitting soft ground instead of ice. "Larry, you okay?" Sarah's voice called out, distant but concerned. I looked up and froze.

When we crossed through the mysterious veil, it was as if we had stepped into another dimension—a place where the rules of the Earth we thought we knew had no longer applied. The air was warmer, almost tropical, despite the icy peaks that loomed in every direction. The Guardians had bid us farewell at the edge of the veil, their cryptic warnings about what lay beyond echoing in my mind. Without their guidance, we ventured forward, curiosity outweighing caution. The journey was slow at first. The terrain was unfamiliar and treacherous, with jagged ice formations and stretches of snow-covered ground that seemed to shift underfoot. The light here was different, almost ethereal, casting everything in a faint bluish glow. The stillness was unnerving, broken only by the crunch of our boots on the ice and the occasional gust of wind.

It wasn't long before we came upon something extraordinary: a massive fissure in the ice, stretching out before us like a colossal scar on the landscape. The crack was flanked by two towering, jagged peaks, almost like natural sentinels guarding whatever lay beyond. As we approached, the sheer scale of it became apparent. It wasn't just a crack—it was a pathway, a deep and narrow canyon that seemed to lead to some hidden realm. Dr. Harrison was the first to notice the faint shimmer at the bottom of the fissure. "Water," he said. Then we peered over the edge, and there it was—an unknown ocean, its dark surface glinting like obsidian under the strange light. Waves lapped gently against the icy walls, creating a sound that was both familiar and alien. "An ocean... beneath the ice?" Sarah murmured, her voice tinged with disbelief. "It's not just an ocean," Harrison said, his voice tight with excitement. "This changes everything. If there's liquid water here, there's a possibility of life—" His words were cut off by a sudden, guttural squawk that echoed through the canyon. We froze, the sound sending a chill down my spine. Before we could react, shadows moved in the periphery of our vision.

Then out of the fissure emerged creatures unlike anything I had ever seen: penguins, but massive—standing at least 2.5 meters tall. Their bodies were covered in sleek black feathers that shimmered faintly, and their beady eyes glinted with a predatory intensity. These were not the cute, waddling birds I had grown up seeing on nature documentaries. These were hunters. "They're coming this way!" Sarah shouted, her voice laced with panic. Then we turned to run, but our boots kept slipping on the ice as the creatures charged. Their speed was terrifying; despite their size, they moved with an agility that belied their bulk. Their sharp beaks clacked together with unsettling precision, and their wings—larger and more powerful than those of any ordinary penguin—flapped furiously, propelling them forward. "Move! Don't stop!" Harrison yelled, his voice barely hearable over the pounding of my own heart.

Then we scrambled down the icy pathway, the massive penguins hot on our trail. As we neared the edge of the unknown ocean, the ground leveled out slightly, giving us just enough of an advantage to put a bit of distance between us and our pursuers. "Over here!" Drew shouted, pointing to a cluster of jagged ice formations near the shoreline. We ducked behind them, gasping for breath as the creatures halted their chase, stopping a few meters away. They paced back and forth, their eyes fixed on us, as if deciding whether to continue the pursuit. "What the hell are those things?" I asked, my voice hoarse. "Predators," Harrison said grimly. "And they're not from any ecosystem I've ever studied." The creatures eventually retreated, their forms disappearing back into the fissure. But the relief was short-lived. Then Harrison pulled out a satellite phone from his pack, his hands trembling as he dialed a number. "This is Dr. Alan Harrison," he said when the call connected. "I need to report a major discovery. We've found an ocean—an entirely unknown ecosystem. Coordinates transmitting now."

Then there was a pause as the person on the other end of the line responded. Harrison's face, already pale, seemed to lose what little color it had left. "What do you mean, we're not on the Earth as you know it?" he asked, his voice barely above a whisper. The rest of us stared at him, confused and alarmed.

Harrison listened for another moment, then he lowered the phone, his expression a mix of shock and disbelief. "They said we've passed through the Sentinels' Gate," he said, his voice shaking. "We're... we're not on Earth as we know it anymore. This place... it's called Atlas."

The words hung in the air, heavy and incomprehensible. My mind reeled, struggling to grasp the enormity of what he had just said. Not on Earth? How was that even possible because we did not get in a spaceship? "So... this is another world?" Sarah asked. Harrison nodded. "That's what they're telling me. The veil we passed through—it's some kind of dimensional boundary. The Guardians knew about this, didn't they? That's why they stayed behind."

I looked out at the dark, shimmering ocean, its waves crashing softly against the icy shore. The air felt heavier now, as if the very fabric of this place carried a weight we weren't meant to understand. This wasn't just an expedition anymore. This was something far greater—far more dangerous—than anything we had prepared for. And as we stood there, staring out at the unknown, a single thought echoed in my mind: What have we gotten ourselves into?

So on the following day it dawned with an eerie quietness, the kind of silence that comes before something life-changing. We awoke, still grappling with the revelation that we were no longer on Earth but in a world called Atlas. The strange ocean stretched endlessly before us, shimmering under the alien sky. And none of us had any appetite for breakfast as we tried to wrap our heads around the sheer scale of what was happening. Then it happened and it was midmorning when we saw it: a boat approaching from the vast unknown ocean. At first, it looked like a black dot on the horizon, bobbing along the gentle waves. But slowly, it grew larger, and we began to make out its shape. It was unlike any vessel I had seen before—sleek and almost futuristic, with a faint glow emanating from its sides.

The boat came to a smooth halt at the icy shoreline, and a man stepped out. He was dressed in a sharp black coat and sunglasses, his presence radiating authority. He introduced himself simply as Agent Maddox, but there was no mistaking who he represented. "Dr. Harrison, Mr. Bridge, team," Maddox said, his voice calm but commanding. "You've done well to come this far. The agency has been monitoring your progress since you entered the Sentinels' Gate. I'm here to take you to the next phase of this mission." "What next phase?" Sarah asked, her voice tinged with both curiosity and skepticism. Maddox gave a faint smile. "You've discovered the Atlas Ocean, but what lies beyond it is even more extraordinary. Get on the boat, and you'll see for yourselves." There wasn't much discussion. Whether it was curiosity or trust in the chain of command, we followed Maddox onto the boat. Its interior was as sleek as its exterior, with high-tech controls and seats that adjusted to our comfort as we sat. Maddox took the helm, his hands steady on the controls.

Then as the boat glided across the dark waters, the sense of unease I had been carrying since we passed through the veil began to wane, replaced by a growing sense of wonder. The waves lapped against the hull with a hypnotic rhythm, and the glow from the ocean's surface cast strange reflections on the boat's interior. "Where exactly are we going?" I finally asked Maddox after an hour of silence. "To a continent known as Min and Mnevis," Maddox replied, his tone matter-of-fact. "It's one of the most biologically diverse regions of Atlas. You'll see things there that defy everything you know about life on Earth. But remember, nothing here is what it seems." He said no more, leaving us to sit in silence and ponder his cryptic words.

The journey lasted hours, maybe even a full day—it was hard to tell time under Atlas's alien sky. The ocean seemed endless, but eventually, we saw land rising on the horizon. It was like nothing I had ever seen. Towering formations of what appeared to be coral lined the shoreline, their colors shifting in the light like a living kaleidoscope. And as we drew closer, the strangeness of the landscape became more apparent. The "trees" looked like animals—long, sinewy structures that swayed and pulsed as if breathing. Their limbs stretched toward the sky, curling and uncurling like tentacles. And then there were the "animals," which resembled plants in every way. They were stationary, rooted to the ground, their surfaces covered in patterns that mimicked leaves and bark. "What... what is this place?" Drew whispered, his voice filled with awe. "Welcome to Min and Mnevis," Maddox said as the boat slowed to a halt at the shore. "This is a continent where evolution took an entirely different path. What you're seeing are examples of convergent mimicry. Life here developed to blur the lines between flora and fauna."

Then we stepped off the boat cautiously, with our boots sinking slightly into the soft, moss-like ground. And the air was thick with a sweet, earthy aroma, and the sounds of the "forest" were unlike anything I had ever heard—a low hum, almost like a symphony, made up of countless small noises. Dr. Harrison knelt down to examine one of the stationary "animals." It was green, with fronds resembling leaves extending from its body, but when he touched it, it shuddered and emitted a low, guttural sound. "It's alive," Harrison murmured, his eyes wide with excitement. "But it's... a plant? Or is it an animal?" "It's both," Maddox said. "And neither. You'll find that categories like 'plant' and 'animal' don't hold much meaning here. Life on Min and Mnevis evolved to adapt to its environment in ways that Earth's life never could."

So as we ventured further inland, the landscape grew even stranger. We passed by "forests" where the "trees" swayed and turned to face us as we walked. Some of them even seemed to emit low, melodic sounds, as if communicating with each other. At one point, we encountered a group of creatures that resembled massive, glowing flowers. They appeared to be rooted to the ground, but as we approached, they suddenly uprooted themselves and began to move, their glowing petals undulating like jellyfish. "This is incredible," Sarah said, her voice filled with wonder. "It's like stepping into a dream." But it wasn't all wonder and beauty. The further we went, the more we began to notice signs of danger. Maddox warned us to steer clear of certain areas where the "plants" emitted strange, pungent odors. "That's a defense mechanism," he explained. "Those species release toxins to deter predators—or intruders."

The realization that even the plant-like creatures could be deadly added an edge of caution to our exploration. So by the time we reached what Maddox referred to as the "heart" of Min and Mnevis—a massive clearing filled with glowing, pulsating structures that looked like a combination of coral and fungi—I felt like I had stepped into another world entirely. "This is just the beginning," Maddox said as he gestured to the alien landscape around us. "What you're seeing here is only a fraction of what Atlas has to offer. And this continent holds secrets that could change humanity's understanding of life itself." Then as I stood there, surrounded by the impossible beauty and danger of Min and Mnevis, I couldn't help but feel both exhilarated and overwhelmed. This wasn't just an expedition anymore. This was the beginning of a journey that would challenge everything we thought we knew about life, survival, and the universe itself. Then Agent Maddox left us in a helicopter and we continued on our journey.

Then as we continued our journey the land beyond the Veil was still nothing short of paradise. Gone was the endless expanse of ice and snow we once knew; and in its place was a lush, vibrant city that seemed to defy all logic. Towering structures of crystalline material rose into the sky, their surfaces reflecting the light of twin suns that hung low on the horizon. Rivers of glowing blue water wound their way through the city, and trees with iridescent leaves swayed gently in a warm, fragrant breeze. "I don't believe it," Harrison muttered, his usual stoicism giving way to awe. "It's beautiful," Sarah said. For once, I couldn't find words.

So as we ventured further into the city, we realized it wasn't uninhabited. People—human-like but unmistakably different—emerged from the structures, their movements graceful and deliberate. They were tall and slender, with pale, luminous skin and eyes that seemed to glow softly in the light. Their clothing was intricate and flowing, made of materials that shimmered like liquid silver. One of them stepped forward, a woman with striking features and long, flowing hair that seemed to ripple like water. She regarded us with a mixture of curiosity and caution. "Travelers," she said, her voice melodic yet commanding. "You have crossed the Veil. Few have done so."

Harrison stepped forward, his usual wariness softened by the awe of the moment. "We're explorers. We mean no harm." The woman studied us for a moment longer, then nodded. "Welcome to Elora," she said.

Then as the days passed, we learned more about the city and its people, whom we came to know as the Elorans. They were descendants of the same extraterrestrial civilization as the Guardians, but while the Guardians had chosen to remain in isolation, the Elorans had built a thriving society hidden from the rest of the world. Their technology was centuries ahead of ours, yet their way of life was deeply rooted in harmony with their environment. They cultivated floating gardens, harvested energy from the twin suns, and lived in symbiosis with the strange and beautiful creatures that roamed the land. For me, however, the most captivating discovery was Angel. I first saw her in one of the city's great arboretums, a sprawling sanctuary of vibrant plants and cascading waterfalls. She was tending to a cluster of glowing flowers, her hands moving with a gentle precision that seemed to breathe life into the plants. Something about her stopped me in my tracks. Maybe it was her quiet grace, or the way her laughter carried through the air like a melody. Whatever it was, I found myself drawn to her, unable to look away.

"Larry, you coming?" Sarah called, already moving ahead with the others. "I'll catch up," I said. Then Angel looked up, her glowing eyes meeting mine. For a moment, neither of us spoke. Then, she smiled—a small, hesitant smile that made my heart skip a beat. "You're one of the travelers," she said, her voice soft but warm. I nodded, suddenly feeling self-conscious. "And you're... one of the Elorans?" She laughed, a sound that seemed to lighten the air around us. "Yes, though we don't often meet people like you. I'm Angel." "Larry," I managed, my voice catching slightly. "It's nice to meet you."

Then over the next few days, Angel and I grew closer. She showed me parts of the city that even the Guardians hadn't mentioned—hidden gardens, underground caverns filled with bioluminescent crystals, and ancient halls inscribed with the history of her people. Her curiosity about Earth matched my fascination with Elora. We spent hours talking, exchanging stories and learning from each other. "There's so much beauty in your world," she said one evening as we sat by a glowing river. "But also so much pain. I can see it in your eyes." I looked at her, surprised by the depth of her insight. "It's true," I admitted. "But being here... it feels like hope." She reached out then, her fingers brushing against mine. "Perhaps that's why you were brought here. To remember what hope feels like." So by the end of the week, I couldn't deny the feelings that had grown between us. In a world filled with wonders, Angel had become the most extraordinary of all. And though I didn't know what the future held, I knew one thing for certain—I didn't want to face it without her.

Then I noticed that time passed differently in Elora. Days blended into nights, and weeks seemed to stretch endlessly in this vibrant, otherworldly haven. For an entire month, we lived among the Elorans, learning their ways, exploring their city, and experiencing a peace we hadn't known since we first set foot on the Ice. It was a paradise unlike anything I'd ever imagined. Yet, for me, it was more than just the city's beauty or the wonders of its advanced technologies. It was Angel. The Elorans had welcomed us with open arms, but they were cautious in their approach, revealing their secrets in small increments. We attended gatherings in the grand halls where their leaders spoke of their history, and we marveled at displays of their technology that made even the most advanced human inventions seem primitive. But my favorite moments were the quieter ones, spent with Angel. She had become my guide, not just through the physical city but through its heart and soul.

Then one morning, as the twin suns cast a golden glow across the crystalline buildings, Angel took me to the highest point in the city—a terrace that overlooked the entirety of Elora. The view was breathtaking. Rivers of blue light wove through the city like veins, and the trees with their shimmering leaves seemed to glow in the sunlight. "This is where I come to think," she said, her voice soft. I looked at her, her face radiant in the light. "What do you think about?" She smiled, a hint of sadness in her eyes. "About the balance we've managed to keep here. About the dangers of what lies beyond. And now... about you."

Our connection grew in ways I couldn't have anticipated. Angel wasn't just beautiful—she was kind, intelligent, and endlessly curious. She wanted to know everything about Earth, about my life, about what it meant to be human in a world so different from hers. So in return, she opened up about her own life, her fears, her dreams. She spoke of the challenges her people faced, the delicate balance they maintained to preserve their paradise, and her own longing to see what lay beyond the Ice.

So one evening, as we walked along the glowing river that wound through the city, I felt compelled to ask. "Do you ever think about leaving this place?" I said. Angel looked at me, her glowing eyes thoughtful. "Sometimes," she admitted. "But this is my home. My people need me." Her words struck a chord. I realized then that I wasn't just falling for her—I was falling for everything she represented. The others noticed, of course. Sarah teased me relentlessly, though always with a smile. Harrison was more reserved, but even he couldn't hide his smirk whenever he saw Angel and me together. "She's good for you, Larry," Sarah said one night as we sat by one of the city's glowing fountains. "I don't think I've ever seen you this happy." I didn't respond, but I couldn't help the smile that spread across my face.

And the month in Elora wasn't without its challenges. The Elorans had rules, boundaries we had to respect. And some parts of the city were off-limits, and there were questions they wouldn't answer, no matter how hard we pushed. But despite the occasional tension, there was an undeniable sense of mutual respect between us. The Elorans were fascinated by our resilience, our ingenuity, and our drive to explore. In turn, we were in awe of their harmony, their wisdom, and the beauty of their world. Angel and I spent more time together than ever. She showed me hidden parts of the city—the underground gardens where plants glowed softly in the dark, the crystal caves that resonated with a strange, haunting music, the ancient library filled with holographic texts that told even more stories of her people.

Then one night, as we sat on the terrace beneath the twin moons, she turned to me, her expression serious. "Larry," she said. "what happens when you leave?" The question caught me off guard. I looked at her, searching for the right words. "I don't know," I admitted. "I hadn't thought that far ahead." She nodded, her gaze distant. "This place... it's all I've ever known. But you... you've seen so much. You've lived in a world I can only imagine." "And yet," I said, taking her hand, "I've never felt more alive than I do here. With you." She smiled then, a small, bittersweet smile that stayed with me long after the moment had passed. Then by the end of the month, Elora felt like home. The city's beauty, its wonders, its people—all of it had become a part of me. But it was Angel who had truly captured my heart. I didn't know what the future held, but one thing was certain: leaving this place, leaving her, would be the hardest thing I'd ever done.

(Echoes of Eden)

The next day when I decided to stay behind in Elora, it wasn't a decision I made lightly. Leaving the team felt like I was tearing away a piece of myself—a piece tied to the life I had always known. But the pull of this place, and of Angel, was stronger than anything I'd ever felt. Elora was a world of wonders, and Angel was its brightest star. I couldn't walk away. The day I told Sarah and Harrison was bittersweet. "You're staying?" Sarah's voice trembled with disbelief, though her expression softened when she saw the conviction in my eyes. I nodded. "This is where I'm supposed to be, Sarah. You know it as well as I do." Harrison crossed his arms, his usual stoicism intact. "And what about the mission? The research? You're just going to walk away?" "I'm not walking away," I said. "I'm walking toward something new. Something I can't leave behind." Then the tension broke when Sarah wrapped me in a hug, her warmth easing the guilt that had settled in my chest. "We'll miss you, Larry. But I get it. She's special. This place is special." Harrison didn't say much after that, but his firm handshake and rare smile spoke volumes.

Then the days that followed felt like the beginning of a new chapter in my life—a chapter I hadn't anticipated but embraced wholeheartedly. Angel and I began carving out a life together in Elora, a life filled with both quiet moments of intimacy and the ever-present awe of living in a world so vastly different from the one I'd left behind. We moved into one of the smaller dwellings on the outskirts of the city, a crystalline structure nestled among towering trees that glowed softly at night. The home was unlike anything I'd ever seen—its walls were semi-transparent, shifting hues with the changing light, and the interior was a seamless blend of nature and technology. "This is yours now," Angel said as we stood in the main room, her eyes bright with excitement. "Ours," I corrected, pulling her close.

So still the decision to stay behind in Elora with Angel was not one I made lightly. Watching my team disappear into the distance, leaving me in this surreal world that defied every law of nature and logic, I felt both liberated and deeply uncertain. But the thought of staying with Angel, to learn more about her and the mysteries of this realm, made the choice an obvious one. Life in Elora was something I could have never imagined—its breathtaking beauty, its harmonious coexistence with nature, its people living in unity with their environment. Yet, despite its wonder, Angel had hinted at something even more incredible waiting beyond the boundaries of her city.

Then on the evening of my third day in Elora, Angel led me to a hidden chamber deep beneath the city. The path to the chamber was a winding series of crystalline tunnels that seemed to hum with energy as we passed through. Finally, we arrived at a circular room, illuminated by a pale blue light emanating from its centerpiece: a tall, intricately designed obelisk-like structure covered in glyphs and symbols that glowed faintly. "What is this?" I asked, unable to mask my awe. Angel smiled, her eyes twinkling with excitement. "It's a teleportation device, Larry. The Sentinels built these long ago to connect the lands of Atlas. Few Elorans even know about it, but it's still functional. I thought you might want to see something... different." "Different?" I repeated, my voice thick with curiosity and trepidation. "You've seen Elora and some of Atlas, but there's a place I think you'd find fascinating—a land called Pitatia. It's unlike anything in your world or mine. Trust me." I hesitated only for a moment before nodding. At this point, I had already crossed so many thresholds of the impossible that stepping into yet another unknown didn't feel as daunting as it should have.

Angel placed her hands on the obelisk and began pressing specific glyphs, her movements deliberate and practiced. The glyphs lit up one by one, and the room filled with a low, resonant hum. Suddenly, a circular portal of shimmering blue light opened before us. "Ready?" Angel asked, holding out her hand. "Ready as I'll ever be," I replied, taking her hand. The sensation of stepping through the portal was indescribable—a mixture of weightlessness and being pulled in every direction at once. When the light cleared, I found myself standing in a place that seemed plucked straight from a prehistoric Earth. Pitatia.

The air was thick and humid, carrying the earthy scent of damp vegetation. Towering ferns and trees stretched toward the sky, their leaves so large they could have shaded an entire house. The ground was a mixture of soft, mossy patches and muddy streams that crisscrossed the landscape. And then, there were the sounds—a cacophony of chirps, growls, and distant roars that filled the air like a symphony of life. "This... this is incredible," I breathed, turning to Angel, who stood beside me with a proud smile. "It's one of my favorite places," she said. "Pitatia is ancient, untouched by the Sentinels' interference. It's a glimpse into what your Earth might have looked like millions of years ago."

So as we ventured further into the swampy terrain, the first creatures we encountered were giant crocodiles lounging near the banks of a wide, slow-moving stream. They were at least three times the size of any crocodile I had seen on Earth, their massive jaws lined with jagged teeth that gleamed in the dappled sunlight. One of them noticed us, its golden eyes locking onto me with unsettling intelligence. It let out a deep, guttural hiss and began to shift its enormous bulk, sliding into the water with a splash that sent ripples across the surface. "Stay back," Angel warned, pulling me gently by the arm. "They're territorial and very dangerous. But if we don't threaten them, they'll leave us alone."

We skirted the edge of the stream, keeping a safe distance from the crocodiles. The further we went, the more life revealed itself. Massive dragonflies, their wings shimmering like stained glass, flitted through the air. Strange, birdlike creatures with scales instead of feathers perched on the branches, their calls echoing through the jungle. And then, I saw them—the lemurs. They were unlike any primates I had ever seen. Standing at human height, they moved with a combination of grace and agility that was mesmerizing. Their fur was a mix of deep browns and grays, with striking patterns that seemed almost too perfect to be natural. They swung effortlessly from the colossal trees, their long arms and prehensile tails allowing them to navigate the dense forest canopy with ease.

And at one point, a pair of them paused on a branch directly above us, their large, curious eyes peering down. One of them tilted its head and let out a series of chittering sounds that seemed almost like laughter. "They're intelligent," Angel explained. "Not quite sentient, but close. They've adapted perfectly to this environment, and their society is incredibly complex for a non-sentient species." "Society?" I asked, glancing up at the lemurs as they continued to observe us. "They work in groups, communicate with intricate vocal patterns, and even use basic tools. They're one of the reasons I love coming here."

We spent hours exploring Pitatia, each new discovery more astonishing than the last. There were towering, carnivorous plants with jaws that snapped shut on unsuspecting insects. Streams filled with glowing fish that swam in perfect synchronization, creating mesmerizing patterns in the water. And everywhere, the sense of a world alive and thriving in its own unique way.

So as time passed it had been only a day since Angel and I returned from the prehistoric wonder of Pitatia, yet I could feel the pull of another adventure lingering in the air. Angel had that look in her eyes again—the one that promised the discovery of something entirely beyond my comprehension. "You've seen the raw, untamed wilderness of Pitatia," she said to me that morning, her tone brimming with excitement. "Now, I want to show you something... different. A place where the rules of reality don't always apply." I raised an eyebrow. "I'm not sure whether to be intrigued or terrified by that description." Angel grinned. "Both would be appropriate."

Then once again, we made our way to the hidden chamber beneath Elora, where the teleportation obelisk awaited. As Angel activated the device, she explained our destination.

"The land is called Zerzura," she said, her fingers gliding over the glowing glyphs. "It's unlike any place in Atlas—or anywhere else, for that matter. Zerzura distorts reality itself. What you see there might not actually be real, and what's real might be impossible to see. But don't worry—I'll be with you." "Comforting," I muttered, though I couldn't deny the thrill of anticipation coursing through me. The portal opened with its familiar hum and glow, and we stepped through together. The first thing I noticed about Zerzura was the sky—or rather, the lack of it. Above us was a swirling expanse of color, a kaleidoscope of hues that shifted and flowed like liquid. It was as if the heavens themselves were alive, constantly moving and changing in ways that defied logic.

And the ground beneath our feet was equally strange. It appeared to be solid, but every step created ripples, as though we were walking on the surface of a pond. Yet, the sensation was firm and stable, as if the ground were merely pretending to be water. "It's beautiful," I said, turning to Angel. "It's also deceptive," she warned. "Zerzura has a way of playing tricks on your mind. Stay close to me." So as we ventured further into this surreal landscape, the distortions became more pronounced. And at one point, I saw a massive tree in the distance, its branches reaching impossibly high into the swirling sky. But as we approached, the tree began to shrink, its towering form collapsing into a tiny sapling no taller than my knee. I knelt down to inspect it, only to look up and realize the tree was massive once again—its trunk wide enough to house an entire building. "It's not just illusions," Angel explained. "Zerzura bends the fabric of reality itself. It's… unstable. But that instability is what makes it so fascinating." So as we continued, we encountered the inhabitants of Zerzura. At first, I thought I was seeing things—figures moving in the distance, their shapes bizarre and otherworldly. But as they drew closer, I realized they were humanoid… but not human. And they had no heads. Instead, their faces were located on their torsos, where their chests should have been. And eyes blinked, noses flared, and mouths moved in strange, rhythmic patterns that I could only assume were some form of communication. Their bodies were slender and elongated, their limbs graceful and fluid in their movements.

Then one of them approached us, its face staring directly at me from its torso. I felt an involuntary shiver run down my spine, but I forced myself to remain calm. Then the being raised a hand in what seemed to be a gesture of peace. Angel stepped forward, bowing slightly, and spoke in a language I didn't recognize. And the being responded in kind, its voice melodic yet dissonant, as though several tones were layered over one another. "They're called the Zerzurians," Angel explained after the exchange. "They're highly intelligent and deeply attuned to the nature of their land. But they're wary of outsiders." "What did you tell them?" I asked. "That we mean no harm and that we're only here to observe," she said. "They've agreed to let us pass, but we shouldn't linger too long. Zerzura can be... unpredictable." So as the Zerzurians watched us as we moved on, their headless forms blending almost seamlessly into the ever-shifting landscape.

Then the deeper we went, the stranger Zerzura became. Mountains rose and fell before our eyes, rivers flowed backward, and the very air seemed to hum with an otherworldly energy. And at one point, I saw what appeared to be my own reflection walking beside me—but it wasn't in a mirror. The reflection moved independently, mimicking me at times and diverging at others. "Don't interact with it," Angel advised. "Zerzura is testing you. If you engage with its tricks, you might lose yourself." I nodded, keeping my focus on Angel as we pressed on. Eventually, we reached a clearing where the distortions seemed to calm. In the center of the clearing was a massive structure—a pyramid-like formation made of translucent material that glowed faintly in the shifting light. Angel approached it with reverence, placing her hand against its surface. "This is the heart of Zerzura," she said. "It's what keeps the land in balance, even amidst its chaos. The Zerzurians consider it sacred."

I stood in awe, feeling a deep sense of humility in the presence of something so ancient and enigmatic. Then after some time, Angel led me back toward the portal we had used to enter Zerzura. And the journey back was just as surreal as our arrival, but I felt a strange sense of calm amidst the chaos. Zerzura was a land of contradictions, of beauty and danger, of wonder and disorientation. Then when we finally stepped through the portal and returned to Elora, I felt a wave of relief wash over me. The familiar sights and sounds of the city were a welcome reprieve from the mind-bending nature of Zerzura. "Thank you for showing me that," I said to Angel, my voice filled with genuine gratitude. She smiled, her eyes twinkling with the light of a thousand unspoken adventures. "There's so much more to see, Larry. But for now, I think we've earned some rest." Then as we walked through the streets of Elora, I couldn't help but reflect on the incredible journey we had just undertaken. Zerzura was unlike anything I had ever imagined—a place that challenged my perception of reality and left me with a profound sense of wonder. And yet, I knew this was only the beginning.

So after me and Angel rested that night the next morning I noticed that the life in Elora was peaceful but never dull. Each day brought new discoveries, new challenges, and new opportunities to grow. Angel and I spent our mornings exploring the city, learning from its elders, and helping with daily tasks. And one day, she took me to the great learning hall again, a towering structure filled with holographic records and interactive displays. "This is where we also preserve our knowledge," she explained, guiding me through the endless corridors. I marveled at the sheer scope of it all. "It's like a living library," I said, running my hand over one of the glowing panels. Angel smiled. "That's exactly what it is. Our history, our science, our art—it's all here, waiting to be shared."

And in the evenings, we often returned to the terrace where we'd first shared our thoughts about life beyond the Veil. Under the twin moons, we talked about everything—our pasts, our dreams, our fears. "Do you miss Earth?" Angel asked one night, her hand resting gently on mine. "Sometimes," I admitted. "But not in the way I thought I would. The things I miss... they don't compare to what I've found here." She smiled, leaning her head on my shoulder. "I'm glad you stayed." "So am I," I said, meaning it more than ever.

Then as the weeks turned into months, our bond deepened. Angel introduced me to her family and friends, and I began to feel truly accepted by the Elorans. They were curious about me, about the world I came from, but they never made me feel like an outsider. And Angel's parents, in particular, were warm and welcoming. Her father, a stoic but kind man named Kael, took an immediate interest in my stories of Earth, while her mother, Lyra, seemed more focused on the happiness Angel and I shared. "She's never smiled like that before," Lyra said one evening as we shared a meal in their home. "You've brought her joy, Larry. That's a gift." I glanced at Angel, who was laughing with her father across the room, and felt a surge of gratitude. "She's given me just as much," I said softly.

Despite the tranquility of our new life, there were challenges, too. Adapting to Eloran culture wasn't always easy. Their customs were intricate, their technology sometimes baffling. But Angel was patient, guiding me through each misstep with kindness and humor. Then one day, while attempting to help with a farming task in one of the floating gardens, I accidentally triggered a mechanism that sent a cascade of glowing water spilling over the crops. Angel laughed as she rushed to help me fix it, her laughter echoing through the air. "You'll get the hang of it eventually," she teased. I grinned, wiping the water from my face. "I'm a work in progress."

And the love we shared became the anchor of my new life. Every moment with Angel felt like a gift—whether we were walking hand in hand through the city, working side by side in the gardens, or simply sitting together under the stars. And one evening, as we watched the twin moons rise over the horizon, I turned to her, my heart full. "I've never been happier," I said, my voice thick with emotion. Angel smiled, her eyes shimmering in the moonlight. "Neither have I." And in that moment, I knew I'd found my place, my purpose, my home.

So as some more time passed life in Elora settled into a rhythm that felt both familiar and extraordinary. And for another month, Angel and I lived in what could only be described as a dream—a perfect blend of romance, discovery, and peace. Every day brought new wonders, but the heart of it all was our growing love. Mornings began with the soft glow of the twin suns peeking through the crystalline walls of our home. I would wake to find Angel already up, standing by the window with a serene expression on her face as she gazed out at the city. "Good morning," I'd say, my voice thick with sleep as I approached her. She'd turn to me with a smile that could light up the entire world. "Good morning, sleepyhead." We'd share a quiet moment, watching as the city came to life. The glowing rivers sparkled in the sunlight, and the soft hum of Elora's energy filled the air like a gentle melody.

And our days were filled with exploration and collaboration. Angel and I worked together on projects that brought us closer to her people. She taught me more about their technology, which still left me awestruck no matter how much I learned. Then one day, she took me to the archives, where the Elorans stored not only their history but the blueprints of their most advanced inventions. "Come here," she said, beckoning me to a large holographic display. With a wave of her hand, a 3D image of a sleek, glowing vehicle appeared. "This is what we use to traverse the icy wilderness beyond the city." I marveled at the design, running my fingers through the light projection. "It's incredible. And this has been here all this time?" Angel nodded. "There's so much here, Larry. You've only scratched the surface." She wasn't wrong. Every corner of Elora seemed to hold secrets, each more fascinating than the last.

Afternoons often found us wandering the floating gardens or strolling through the vibrant marketplaces where Elorans shared their crafts and stories. Angel loved introducing me to her friends and neighbors, who welcomed me with warmth and curiosity. "Larry!" a young Eloran child called out one day as we passed through the market. He ran up to me, holding a small glowing orb. "Look! I made this!" I crouched down to his level, accepting the orb with a smile. "What is it?" "It's a light orb! It changes colors when you touch it!" Sure enough, the orb shifted from blue to green as I held it. "That's amazing," I said, ruffling his hair. Angel laughed as she watched the interaction. "You're a natural with them," she said, taking my hand as we continued through the market.

Evenings were my favorite part of the day. After the hustle and bustle of the city, Angel and I would retreat to our home, where we could simply be together. Sometimes we'd cook meals using the ingredients from Elora's gardens— strange fruits and vegetables that glowed faintly and tasted like nothing I'd ever had on Earth. And other times, we'd sit on the terrace, watching the twin moons rise and the city lights shimmer below.

Then on one evening, as we sat side by side, I turned to her. "Do you ever think about what might have been if I hadn't come here?" Angel's gaze softened. "I don't like to think about that," she said, taking my hand. "You're here now. That's all that matters." Her words settled in my chest like a warm ember. I couldn't imagine my life without her now. So over the course of the month, our bond grew deeper. Angel shared more of her world with me, and I, in turn, opened up about my past. She was endlessly fascinated by my stories of Earth—of bustling cities, vast oceans, and the stars that seemed so far away from here. "You must miss it," she said one night as we lay in bed, her head resting on my chest. "Not as much as I thought I would," I admitted, running my fingers through her hair. "Earth was... home, but it never felt like this." She smiled against my skin. "I'm glad you feel that way." We faced challenges, too. Because living among the Elorans wasn't always seamless. There were cultural differences, misunderstandings, and moments when I felt like an outsider. But Angel was always there to guide me, to bridge the gap between my world and hers.

So on one particularly frustrating day, I struggled to understand a piece of Eloran technology during a community project. And my impatience got the better of me, and I snapped at one of the elders who was trying to help. Later that evening, Angel gently brought it up. "You were frustrated," she said, her voice calm. "It happens. But the Elorans are patient, Larry. They understand you're still learning." Her kindness humbled me, and I resolved to do better. So by the end of the month, I felt more connected to Elora than ever before. And the city was no longer just a place of wonder—it was home. And Angel wasn't just the woman I loved; she was my partner, my anchor, my future. And then one night, as we stood on the terrace under the light of the twin moons, I held her close and whispered the words that had been on my mind for weeks. "I love you, Angel." She looked up at me, her glowing eyes filled with emotion. "I love you too, Larry." And in that moment, surrounded by the beauty of Elora and the warmth of her embrace, I knew I had found everything I'd ever been searching for.

(The White Abyss)

The next morning Angel told me that she wanted to visit Earth and that was one thing I'll never forget. The twin suns were just rising, casting a golden glow over Elora, but her words brought a weight that turned the air cold around us. "I want to see it for myself," she said, her voice soft yet determined as we sat on the terrace. Her eyes, usually so filled with warmth, were now focused with a mixture of curiosity and conviction. "Your world. Earth. I need to understand it the way you understand mine." I blinked, stunned. Of all the conversations we'd had about Earth—about its beauty, its flaws, and its mysteries—I'd never imagined this moment. "Angel," I began cautiously, "it's not like Elora. Earth has its wonders, but it's... harsher. Messier. Are you sure?" She reached for my hand, her touch grounding me. "I know. But I also know that you and I aren't so different. If your people could see what I've seen—what you've seen—it could change everything." Her words struck a chord deep within me. She was right. The knowledge of Elora could reshape humanity's future. But the thought of her stepping into my world, where so much could go wrong, filled me with both hope and dread.

So later that day, I reunited with the research team. They had returned from their latest expedition, their faces weathered by the cold but lit with the fire of discovery. "You're alive!" Sarah exclaimed, throwing her arms around me as soon as she saw me. "We were starting to think you'd vanished into thin air!" Harrison followed close behind, his usual stoic expression cracking just enough to show relief. "Glad to see you in one piece, Bridge. Where's your... companion?" I glanced back toward Angel, who was standing a few paces away, her elegant form wrapped in a cloak of shimmering fabric. She approached slowly, her presence commanding attention. "She's here," I said, smiling as Angel nodded politely to the team. Sarah's eyes widened. "You weren't kidding about her, were you?" "Not even a little," I replied.

And as we settled into the research station later that evening, I explained Angel's desire to visit Earth. The team was skeptical at first, but as Angel spoke, her passion and sincerity began to sway them. "What if Elora's technology could help Earth?" she asked, her voice steady but impassioned. "What if we could bridge our worlds?" Harrison leaned back in his chair, arms crossed. "And what if the rest of the world isn't ready for this? You're talking about a seismic shift, Angel. There are people who won't take kindly to it." "Which is why we have to try," she said. "The longer we stay divided, the more we lose." Her words hung in the air, heavy with meaning. It wasn't just about science or exploration anymore. This was about something much larger.

So the decision to leave Elora didn't sit well with everyone. While most of the city supported Angel's choice, there was one voice of dissent that couldn't be ignored: Nivrek, one of the Guardians. "You don't understand the risks," he said, his tone sharp as he confronted us the next morning. His silver eyes bore into mine with an intensity that made my stomach churn. "A union between an Eloran and a human could disrupt the balance. The consequences could be catastrophic." Angel stood firm, her gaze unwavering. "The only balance I see is one rooted in fear. It's time for change, Nivrek. You can't stop it." The tension between them was palpable, but Nivrek said no more. Instead, he turned and left, his departure heavy with foreboding.

Then we began our journey across the icy wilderness the next day. And the Guardians provided us with supplies and guidance, but their unease lingered like a shadow over our departure. The icy expanse stretched endlessly before us, a stark contrast to the warmth of Elora. The team moved cautiously, their every step marked by the crunch of snow and the howling of the wind. Angel stayed close to me, her hand wrapped tightly around mine. "It's beautiful in its own way," she said, her breath visible in the freezing air. "Yeah," I replied, though my eyes kept scanning the horizon for any signs of danger.

And as we made camp that night, the temperature dropped to an unbearable low. The wind screamed through the wilderness, and the skies darkened ominously. "I don't like this," Harrison muttered, tightening the straps on the tent. "Something's wrong." He was right. Because by morning, the storm had arrived. The blizzard descended on us with a ferocity I'd never experienced before. The winds were so strong they knocked us off our feet, and the snow was blinding, making it impossible to see more than a few feet ahead. "Everyone stay close!" I shouted. Angel clung to my side, her face pale but determined. "We have to find shelter!" We stumbled forward, each step a battle against the elements. The cold seeped through our layers of clothing, biting at our skin and numbing our limbs. "This isn't natural," Sarah yelled, her voice filled with fear. "It's like the storm is targeting us!" Her words sent a chill through me that had nothing to do with the weather. Deep down, I knew she was right. This storm wasn't just a freak occurrence. It was something else—something deliberate. Then hours passed, and the situation grew dire. One of the sleds carrying our supplies was blown over, scattering its contents into the snow. The team was exhausted, their movements sluggish and uncoordinated. "We're not going to make it," Harrison said, his tone grim. "Yes, we are," I snapped, refusing to give in to despair. "We have to." Angel's grip on my arm tightened. "Larry, look!" she shouted, pointing to a faint glow in the distance. It was a cave, its entrance barely visible through the swirling snow. Without hesitation, we made our way toward it, stumbling and falling but refusing to give up. And by the time we reached the cave, we were on the brink of collapse. The warmth of the sheltered space was a small mercy, but it wasn't enough to ease the dread that had settled over us.

So as we huddled together, the reality of our situation sank in. We were trapped in the middle of the icy wilderness, cut off from Elora and the world beyond. The storm raged outside, relentless and unyielding. Angel leaned against me, her body trembling from the cold. "This isn't over," she whispered". "No," I agreed, wrapping my arms around her. "It's just beginning." Deep down, I knew the adversary wasn't done with us. And as I stared into the flickering firelight, I realized that our journey was about to take a much darker turn.

And the blizzard had not relented. It howled with a ferocity that made it seem alive, as though some unseen force were determined to keep us trapped. Day after day, the storm raged on, burying the landscape in endless layers of snow and ice. I sat huddled near the fire we had managed to maintain in the small cave that had become our temporary refuge. The flickering light painted shadows on the jagged walls, but it did little to dispel the oppressive cold that gnawed at our bones. Angel was curled up beside me, her head resting on my shoulder. Her strength amazed me; even now, after days of this relentless siege, she hadn't let despair take her. "What time is it?" Sarah asked, her voice hoarse. She was sitting on the other side of the fire, her hands trembling as she tried to warm them. "Does it matter?" Harrison replied, his tone bitter. He had been sharpening a small knife for the better part of an hour, the repetitive scrape of metal against stone filling the silence between the storm's howls. "Day, night—it's all the same out there. Just more of this damn blizzard." I sighed, shifting slightly to ease the ache in my back. "It's been a week," I said quietly. "At least, I think it has." The team had stopped counting days in the conventional sense. Without the sun to mark the passage of time, everything blurred together. The only thing we knew for certain was that we were alive—for now.

And the food supply was dwindling. So we had rationed carefully, but the cold burned through calories faster than we could afford. But water wasn't an issue; we could melt snow for that. But the lack of sustenance was beginning to show. "I'm going out," Harrison announced suddenly, standing and grabbing his coat. "No, you're not," I said firmly. He glared at me. "We need more wood for the fire. If this goes out, we're done." I glanced at the meager pile of branches and broken planks we had scavenged before the storm intensified. He wasn't wrong—we were running low. But the thought of anyone venturing out into that nightmare was unbearable. "I'll go with you," I said, rising to my feet. "No," Angel said sharply, grabbing my arm. Her eyes, wide with fear, locked onto mine. "You can't. It's too dangerous." I cupped her face gently, my thumb brushing her cheek. "I'll be careful. I promise."

Harrison and I bundled up as best we could, layering every piece of clothing we had. The moment we stepped outside, the wind slammed into us with a force that nearly knocked us off our feet. Snow swirled around us, reducing visibility to mere inches. "Stay close!" I shouted over the roar of the storm. Harrison nodded, and we pressed forward, moving slowly and deliberately. The cold was like a living thing, seeping through every crack and crevice, biting at our exposed skin. We managed to find a few pieces of wood buried beneath the snow, remnants of some long-forgotten structure. It wasn't much, but it was something.

And on the way back, I thought I saw movement in the distance—a shadowy figure, fleeting and indistinct. I stopped, squinting against the snow. "What is it?" Harrison asked. "I don't know," I replied, my heart pounding. "Probably nothing." But as we returned to the cave, I couldn't shake the feeling that we were being watched. Inside, the atmosphere was tense. Angel rushed to my side as soon as I entered, her hands brushing snow from my coat. "You're freezing," she said, her voice filled with worry. "I'm fine," I assured her, though my body ached from the cold. Sarah and Harrison worked quickly to add the wood to the fire, coaxing the flames back to life. The warmth was a small comfort, but it wasn't enough to erase the growing sense of dread that hung over us. "We can't keep this up," Sarah said, her voice trembling. "If the storm doesn't end soon..." She didn't finish the sentence, but she didn't need to. We all knew what would happen.

That night, as the others tried to sleep, Angel and I sat together, our backs against the cave wall. "I've never seen Nivrek this angry," she said softly. "He warned us, Larry. He warned us about what could happen." Her words sent a shiver down my spine. Nivrek's disapproval of our relationship—and of Angel's desire to visit Earth—had been clear from the start. But could he really be behind this? Could he wield such power over the elements? "It doesn't matter," I said, my voice steady. "We'll get through this. Together." She looked at me, her eyes shining with unshed tears. "I hope you're right."

Then the next day, we discovered something unsettling. One of the Guardians' beacons, a device meant to guide us through the wilderness, had been smashed. It was buried in the snow not far from the cave, its intricate components shattered beyond repair. "This wasn't an accident," Harrison said grimly, holding up a piece of the broken device. "Someone doesn't want us to leave," Sarah added, her voice shaking. Angel's expression hardened. "It's Nivrek. I know it is." Her certainty sent a ripple of unease through the group. If the Guardians were truly working against us, our chances of survival were even slimmer than we thought.

So as the week dragged on, the storm showed no signs of stopping. The blizzard had become a constant presence, a relentless force that seemed determined to break us. But even in the darkest moments, there were small glimmers of hope.

Angel and I grew closer, our bond strengthened by the shared struggle. And despite the odds, the team refused to give up. "We've come this far," I said one night as we sat around the fire. "We're not going to let a little snow stop us." Sarah laughed bitterly. "A little snow? Larry, this is a full-blown apocalypse." "Maybe," I admitted. "But we're still here. And as long as we're alive, there's a chance." Angel smiled faintly, her hand slipping into mine. "He's right. We can't give up." Her words were a beacon in the darkness, a reminder that even in the face of overwhelming odds, hope could still shine through.

(The Bonds of Survival)

After a few days the storm finally broke after what felt like an eternity, the howling winds quieted, and the relentless snow finally stopped its assault. Then when I emerged from the cave, I was met with a stillness so profound it made my ears ring. The world was unrecognizable—a desolate expanse of white, stretching endlessly in every direction. For the first time in weeks, the sun broke through the clouds, its light dazzling as it reflected off the snow-covered landscape. The sight should have brought relief, but instead, it reminded me of how far we were from safety. Behind me, Angel stepped out into the open, shielding her eyes against the glare. "It's beautiful," she said softly. "It is," I agreed. But beauty didn't change the fact that we were still stranded in the middle of nowhere, with miles of treacherous wilderness between us and the research station.

And inside the cave, the team was already preparing to move. Harrison packed what little gear we had left, his movements quick and efficient. Sarah was studying the map, though much of it was now useless after the blizzard had reshaped the terrain. "We'll head east," she said, pointing to a rough estimate of our current location. "If we keep a steady pace, we should reach the station in three days." "Three days if we don't run into any more surprises," Harrison muttered. "No choice," I said, tightening the straps on my pack. "We either move now, or we stay here and hope for another miracle. I'm not betting on the latter." And the first day of the journey was grueling. The snow was deep, and every step felt like wading through quicksand. The sled we used to carry our remaining supplies kept getting stuck, forcing us to stop and dig it out repeatedly. Angel stayed close to me, her presence a source of strength. She wasn't used to this kind of physical exertion, but she never complained. Instead, she pushed forward with a quiet determination that made me admire her even more.

"How are you holding up?" I asked during one of our short breaks. She gave me a tired smile. "I've had better days, but I'll survive. As long as you're with me." Her words warmed me in a way the fire never could. So on the second day, the temperature dropped even further, making the trek even more dangerous. Frost clung to our clothing, and the cold bit through every layer. "We need to keep moving," Harrison said, his breath visible in the frigid air. "Stopping for too long isn't an option." He was right. The cold was a predator, waiting for us to falter. By nightfall, we found a small hollow in the snow where we could set up a makeshift camp. Angel and I huddled together, sharing body heat as we tried to get some rest. "Do you think we'll make it?" she asked "We'll make it," I said firmly. "We've come too far to give up now."

And on the third day, the landscape began to change. The endless flatness gave way to rolling hills, and in the distance, we saw the faint outline of the research station. "There it is!" Sarah shouted, her voice filled with relief. The sight gave us a burst of energy, and we quickened our pace despite our exhaustion. But the journey wasn't over yet. The last stretch was the hardest, with steep inclines and icy patches that made every step a challenge. Halfway up one of the hills, the sled tipped over, spilling its contents into the snow. Harrison cursed, and we scrambled to recover what we could. "Leave it!" I shouted. "We're close enough now. We don't need it." Reluctantly, the others agreed, and we abandoned the sled, carrying only what we could manage.

Then when we finally reached the station, it felt like crossing the finish line of an impossible race. The doors opened, and the warmth inside enveloped us like a long-lost friend. The other researchers rushed to meet us, their faces a mixture of shock and relief. They had assumed the worst when we didn't return after the blizzard hit. "What happened out there?" one of them asked as we collapsed into chairs, too exhausted to speak. "It's a long story," I said, my voice hoarse. "But we're here now. That's what matters."

Later that night, as we sat by the fire, Angel leaned her head against my shoulder. "We made it," she said softly. "We did," I replied, wrapping an arm around her. The ordeal had taken its toll on all of us, but it had also brought us closer together. In those endless days of cold and fear, we had become more than a team—we had become a family. And though the dangers of the icy wilderness still loomed, I knew we could face them. Together. So I noticed that the warmth of the research station was an abrupt contrast to the biting cold we had endured for weeks. Angel stepped through the threshold tentatively, her eyes darting around the interior as if trying to absorb every detail at once. The station wasn't much to look at—metal walls, buzzing fluorescent lights, and a clutter of scientific equipment—but to us, it was home. "You live here?" she asked, her voice a mix of curiosity and disbelief. "For months at a time," I replied. "It's not exactly five-star, but it gets the job done." She smiled faintly, running her fingers along the edge of a stainless-steel table. "It's... different." "It grows on you," I said, trying to mask the awkwardness I felt. Seeing the station through her eyes made me realize how sterile and unwelcoming it appeared. So as the others settled in and began unpacking, I decided to give Angel a tour. "Come on," I said, motioning for her to follow me. "I'll show you around." We started with the common area, a cramped space filled with mismatched chairs and a small coffee table piled with dog-eared books and half-empty mugs. "This is where we unwind," I explained. Angel picked up one of the books, flipping through the pages. "Do you ever have time to relax?" "Not as much as we'd like," I admitted. "Most of the time, we're working or sleeping." She nodded thoughtfully, placing the book back on the table.

Next, I showed her the lab, a sprawling room filled with microscopes, computers, and rows of labeled specimens. Sarah was there, already analyzing samples from our ill-fated expedition. "This is where the magic happens," I said. "Magic?" Angel asked, raising an eyebrow. "Science, magic—it's all the same when you're trying to make sense of the unknown," I joked. Sarah glanced up from her work and offered Angel a warm smile. "Feel free to look around," she said. "Just don't touch anything labeled 'volatile.'" Angel chuckled softly but stayed close to me, her gaze lingering on the intricate machinery. "It's incredible how much you've accomplished here," she said. "It's a team effort," I replied. "None of us could do it alone."

So in the kitchen, I introduced her to the station's less glamorous side: the food. "Freeze-dried everything," I said, holding up a packet of dehydrated spaghetti. She wrinkled her nose. "You actually eat that?" "Every day," I said with mock enthusiasm. "It's not as bad as it looks, but it's definitely not gourmet." "I'll cook for you someday," she said, her tone light but sincere. I smiled, the thought of a home-cooked meal more appealing than ever. "I'll hold you to that."

Then later that day the tour ended in the sleeping quarters, a narrow hallway lined with small, identical rooms. I opened the door to mine, revealing a bed, a desk, and a few personal items scattered around. "This is me," I said. Angel stepped inside, her eyes scanning the space. She picked up a framed photo from the desk—a picture of my family from years ago. "Your family?" she asked. "Yeah," I said, my voice softening. "It's been a while since I've seen them." She placed the photo back carefully, her expression unreadable. "Do you miss them?" "Every day," I admitted. Then there was a moment of silence before she turned to me, her gaze steady. "You're a good man, Larry. They must be proud of you." Her words caught me off guard, and for a moment, I didn't know how to respond. Finally, I managed a quiet, "Thank you."

Over the next few days, Angel became a fixture in the station. She was eager to learn, asking questions about everything from our research methods to the history of the facility. The team welcomed her with open arms, impressed by her intelligence and genuine curiosity. "She's a quick learner," Sarah remarked one evening as we sat in the common area. "You've got yourself a good one, Larry." I couldn't help but smile. "Yeah, I know." Angel, meanwhile, had taken a particular interest in the archives—a room filled with decades' worth of records and data. I found her there one night, poring over an old journal. "What are you up to?" I asked, leaning against the doorframe. "Just trying to understand your world," she said without looking up. "Our world," I corrected gently. She glanced at me, her expression thoughtful. "It's strange, isn't it? How different we are, yet so much alike." "It is," I agreed. "But maybe that's a good thing. It means we can learn from each other." She smiled, setting the journal aside. "I'd like that." So by the end of the week, Angel had become an integral part of our little community. She joined us in the lab, assisted with data analysis, and even managed to cook a meal using the limited ingredients we had. And as I watched her interact with the team, I felt a deep sense of pride. She wasn't just adapting to our world—she was thriving in it. And in her presence, the station felt less like a cold, lifeless building and more like a home.

(Ancient Footprints)

The next day snow crunched beneath our boots as we trekked further into the unknown. The icy wilderness stretched endlessly ahead, its silence broken only by the occasional gust of wind or the muffled voices of the team as they discussed their findings. This was our first major expedition since surviving the blizzard, and though our bodies were still weary, the drive to uncover more secrets of this enigmatic land pushed us onward. Angel walked beside me, her expression a mixture of curiosity and unease. "Are you sure about this, Larry?" she asked, her voice soft but carrying in the still air. "As sure as I can be," I replied, adjusting my pack. "There's something out here. I can feel it." She glanced ahead at the snow-covered horizon, her brow furrowed. "I've lived here my whole life, but this place… it feels different. Like it doesn't belong."

Then we reached the site just before midday. It was Harrison who first spotted the anomaly—a faint outline in the snow that didn't match the natural formations around it. "Over here!" he called, his voice tinged with excitement. The team gathered around as he knelt and began brushing away the snow. Slowly, a pattern emerged—an intricate carving etched into the ice. "It's a glyph," Sarah said, her voice trembling. "But it's not Eloran. This is something else entirely." Angel knelt beside the carving, her fingers tracing the lines with reverence. "I don't recognize it," she admitted, her tone filled with wonder. "This isn't from my people." The realization sent a ripple of shock through the group. If this wasn't Eloran in origin, then who had created it?

The glyphs led us to a series of stone steps, partially buried beneath layers of ice. They descended into the earth at a sharp angle, their surfaces worn smooth by time. "Looks like we're going down," I said, my voice steady despite the apprehension building in my chest. "Are we sure that's a good idea?" Sarah asked, glancing nervously at the dark entrance below. "We didn't come all this way to turn back now," I replied, stepping forward. "Stay close and watch your footing." Angel placed a hand on my arm as I led the way. "Be careful," she said softly. "I always am," I assured her, though the truth was far less comforting.

And the descent was slow and cautious and the air grew colder the deeper we went, and the faint light from above soon gave way to complete darkness. We relied on our headlamps to illuminate the path, their beams revealing walls covered in more glyphs and carvings. "These symbols…" Angel murmured, running her fingers over one of the carvings. "They tell a story, but it's fragmented. I can't make sense of it." "Take pictures," Harrison suggested, pulling out his camera. "We can analyze them back at the station."

So as we continued, the passage widened, opening into a vast chamber that took my breath away. There was a city laid before us, hidden beneath the ice for what must have been a millennia. Towering spires of crystal and stone reached toward the ceiling, their surfaces glinting faintly in the dim light. The architecture was unlike anything I had ever seen—both alien and hauntingly familiar. "By the stars…" Angel whispered, her voice filled with awe. We spread out cautiously, each of us drawn to different aspects of the city. Sarah examined the intricate mosaics that adorned the walls, while Harrison focused on the machinery scattered throughout the space—devices that defied explanation. Angel stood in the center of the chamber, her gaze fixed on a large obelisk at its heart. "This place… it feels alive," she said. I joined her, placing a hand on her shoulder. "What do you mean?" She shook her head, struggling to find the words. "It's like it's waiting for something—or someone."

So as we explored, we uncovered more mysteries. A series of chambers branching off from the main hall contained artifacts that hinted at an advanced civilization—one that predated even the Elorans. "Look at this," Sarah said, holding up a delicate object that resembled a compass, though its markings were unrecognizable. "It's beautiful." Harrison, meanwhile, discovered a series of tablets covered in glyphs. "If we can translate these, they might give us some answers," he said, carefully packing them into his bag. But not all discoveries were welcome. In one chamber, we found skeletal remains—evidence that this city had once been inhabited, and that something had driven its people to their end. "This doesn't feel right," Angel said, her voice trembling. "We shouldn't be here." I placed a reassuring hand on her arm. "We'll leave soon," I promised. "But we need to understand what this place is."

So as the night fell, we set up a makeshift camp in one of the chambers, lighting a small fire for warmth. The atmosphere was tense, each of us lost in our thoughts. "This changes everything," Sarah said, her voice breaking the silence. "If this city predates Elora, then… what does that mean for us?" "It means we're not alone," Harrison replied. "We've never been alone." Angel sat beside me, her expression unreadable. "I've always believed my people were the first," she said quietly. "But this… it's humbling." "It's a piece of a puzzle," I said, wrapping an arm around her. "And we'll figure it out. Together."

So as the weeks followed our initial discovery were a blur of activity, each day unveiling more layers of the enigmatic city buried beneath the ice. It was as though the city itself wanted to be found, revealing secrets one stone, one glyph, one artifact at a time. The team had taken up residence in a relatively intact chamber near the entrance to the city—a space that provided shelter from the relentless cold. We called it "Base Camp Echo," a fitting name for a place where every whispered word seemed to linger in the air, carried by the acoustics of the ancient walls. Angel and I often found ourselves wandering the city together during the evenings, her insights invaluable as we pieced together the story of this forgotten civilization.

Then one morning, Harrison called us to a site deeper within the city. He stood before a large archway carved into the stone, its surface covered in intricate glyphs that glowed faintly when touched. "This wasn't here before," he said, his voice tinged with both awe and disbelief. I frowned, stepping closer. "How could something like this suddenly appear?" Angel tilted her head, examining the glyphs. "Maybe it was always here, but we didn't know how to see it," she suggested. Sarah, the team's linguist, was already snapping photos and taking notes. "These symbols are different from the others," she observed. "More complex. It's almost as if... they're alive." The archway led to a long corridor, its walls adorned with murals depicting scenes of a vibrant civilization. Figures danced in harmony, their hands raised toward the skies, while others worked with strange devices that seemed to harness the energy of the earth itself. "This city was advanced," Angel said, her voice filled with admiration. "Far more than my people ever were."

So as we ventured deeper, we came across a central plaza dominated by a massive fountain. Though no water flowed, the craftsmanship was breathtaking— intricate carvings of animals, plants, and celestial bodies spiraled up the structure, telling a story we could only begin to comprehend. Harrison crouched near the base of the fountain, studying a series of small, engraved tiles. "These look like they were meant to move," he said, pressing one experimentally. The fountain rumbled, a low vibration that resonated through the ground. The carvings began to glow softly, casting an ethereal light across the plaza. "What did you do?" Sarah asked, her voice a mix of wonder and alarm. "I think I activated something," Harrison replied, stepping back as the fountain continued to hum. Angel reached for my hand, her grip tight. "This city isn't dead, Larry. It's waiting for something—or someone."

Then later that day we discovered more chambers as the days went on, each revealing artifacts that challenged our understanding of history. In one room, we found a series of crystalline orbs that projected images when touched. "These are memories," Angel said, her voice trembling as she watched a scene unfold—a group of people, similar to the Elorans, working together to build the city. "It's like they wanted to preserve their story." Sarah, ever the skeptic, studied one of the orbs closely. "Why would they leave these behind?" she mused aloud. "Did they know their civilization was coming to an end?" "No civilization lasts forever," Angel said softly. "But this one... it feels like it ended too soon."

Then one evening, while exploring a smaller, more secluded chamber, Angel and I stumbled upon what appeared to be a library. Shelves carved into the stone walls held countless tablets and scrolls, each inscribed with glyphs. "This must be where they kept their knowledge," I said, running my fingers along the edge of one of the shelves. Angel picked up a tablet, her eyes scanning the symbols. "These texts... they talk about a great exodus. It says they left the city to escape something, but it doesn't say what." I frowned, the words stirring a sense of unease. "Maybe they were running from the same adversary we're dealing with now." Angel placed the tablet back on the shelf, her expression somber. "If that's true, then we need to be careful. Whatever drove them away might still be out there."

Then back at Base Camp, the team worked tirelessly to catalog everything we had found. Harrison focused on the machinery, attempting to understand its purpose, while Sarah continued her efforts to translate the glyphs. Angel spent her time with the crystalline orbs, piecing together fragments of the city's history. I often joined her, marveling at the images they projected—scenes of a thriving civilization that had once called this frozen wasteland home. "What do you think happened to them?" I asked one evening, as we watched an orb display a group of people gathered around a glowing artifact. Angel shook her head. "I don't know. But I feel like we're getting closer to the truth." Then the city revealed its secrets reluctantly, as if testing our resolve. Some days were filled with breakthroughs, while others left us frustrated and questioning why we were there. But through it all, we pressed on, driven by a shared determination to uncover the truth. For me, the journey was about more than just discovery. It was about Angel—the way her eyes lit up when she deciphered a new clue, the way her voice trembled with emotion as she spoke of her people's connection to this place. "This city has changed you," I told her one evening, as we sat together near the fountain. She smiled, her gaze fixed on the glowing carvings. "It's changed all of us," she replied. "But I think it's only the beginning."

(The Ice Chronicles)

The next day the Guardians gathered us in the grand chamber of their council hall, a cavernous space deep within the Ice City where every surface shimmered with crystalline frost that seemed to pulse with an inner light. The air was heavy with anticipation as we took our seats in a semi-circle around them. They stood like statues, their silver robes flowing as if moved by an unseen breeze, their expressions solemn yet inviting. "This will take time," the elder Guardian, Amara, began, her voice resonating as though amplified by the very walls of the chamber. "But if you are to understand the gravity of your presence here, you must know the full story of this land." Angel squeezed my hand, her eyes reflecting a mixture of curiosity and unease. I nodded at her reassuringly. We were about to learn something monumental.

Amara raised her hand, and the icy walls of the chamber began to glow. Images formed in the frost—vast, shifting landscapes of green plains and towering mountains. "Antarctica was not always a land of ice," she began. "Eons ago, it was a paradise, a thriving hub of life where the first civilizations on this planet arose. The land was warm, its rivers teeming with life, its skies clear and vibrant." She showed us a vision of colossal cities constructed from organic materials, their architecture flowing seamlessly into the natural landscape. These were the Ancients, the first beings to harness the energies of the earth. "They built wonders beyond comprehension," Amara continued. "Cities that could heal themselves, machines that harmonized with the planet's rhythms. They lived in balance, but as with all great civilizations, their unity fractured." The images shifted to scenes of conflict—earthquakes, volcanic eruptions, and floods. "A cataclysm of their own making tore the land apart, and the paradise was lost."

Then with a wave of her hand, Amara transitioned the vision to a stark, frozen landscape. Glaciers advanced, consuming the land as temperatures plummeted. "The Ice came swiftly," she said, her tone heavy. "It was as if the planet itself sought to heal the wounds inflicted upon it. The few who survived fled to other continents, leaving this place to slumber beneath a blanket of snow and frost." Harrison leaned forward, his breath visible in the cold air. "But life returned, didn't it? We've seen evidence of that." Amara nodded. "Indeed. Over a millennia, the Ice receded and advanced in cycles, and with each thaw, new civilizations arose. Some were visitors from your continents; others came from beyond your world." Her words sent a ripple of astonishment through the group. Angel's eyes widened, her grip on my hand tightening.

The next images were breathtaking. Massive ships descended from the heavens, their shapes sleek and unfamiliar. Beings emerged—humanoid, but not entirely like us. They brought knowledge, technology, and an unshakable curiosity about this icy land. "They were not invaders," Amara explained. "They were explorers, much like you. They found Antarctica to be a place of great potential, and they built their own cities here, merging their advanced technology with the remnants of the Ancients' work." Scenes of collaboration appeared—humans and these star-faring beings working side by side. Together, they created wonders that rivaled those of the Ancients. "But their time, too, came to an end," Amara said, her voice tinged with sorrow. "The Ice claimed their cities, their knowledge scattered and buried beneath the frost."

The vision shifted again, showing the familiar silhouettes of wooden ships navigating icy waters. Explorers from Europe appeared, their maps marking the uncharted southern continent. "Your ancestors rediscovered this land during an age of exploration," Amara said. "But they saw it as a desolate wilderness, unaware of the treasures hidden beneath." Images of early expeditions flashed by—men braving the elements, setting up rudimentary camps, and planting flags in the snow. "Then came the modern era," Amara continued. "Nations sought to claim this land for themselves, not realizing its true nature. The Guardians watched, wary of humanity's growing influence." The images transitioned to scenes of diplomats gathered around a table. Documents were signed, treaties forged. "The Antarctic Treaty," Amara said, her tone neutral. "An agreement among your nations to preserve this land for peaceful purposes. But few of you truly understood the depth of what you were protecting."

Amara gestured to her fellow Guardians, who stepped forward, their expressions grave yet serene. "For centuries, we have been the stewards of this land, preserving its secrets and safeguarding its legacy," she said. "We intervened only when necessary, ensuring that no one disturbed the balance." Harrison raised his hand. "Why allow us to be here now? Why reveal all this to us?" Amara's gaze softened. "Because the Ice is changing. Forces beyond our control are at play. The secrets of this land can no longer remain hidden, and you are now part of its story."

So as the images faded and the chamber returned to its natural state, the silence was palpable. Each of us wrestled with the enormity of what we had just learned. "This changes everything," Sarah said finally, "It does," Amara agreed. "But it is up to you to decide what you will do with this knowledge." I looked at Angel, who had been unusually quiet throughout the revelation. Her expression was unreadable, but her eyes held a spark of determination. "What do you think?" I asked her later, as we walked back to our quarters. She sighed, leaning into me. "I think we're standing on the edge of something incredible, Larry. But I also think it's dangerous. Knowledge like this can unite or destroy. We have to be careful." I nodded, her words echoing my own thoughts. The Ice had revealed its story, but the next chapter was ours to write.

So we gathered once more in the council chamber of the Guardians, the icy walls glowing faintly in the dim light. It had been a week since their initial revelations about the history of Antarctica, and while the weight of what we'd learned still hung heavy in our minds, we knew there was more to uncover. The Guardians had summoned us again, offering to share details that hadn't been included in their first account. So I sat next to Angel, her hand resting lightly on my arm, as Amara, the elder Guardian, stepped forward. "We shared with you the broad strokes of this land's history," she began, her voice as measured and resonant as before. "Now we will illuminate the smaller details—truths that may challenge your understanding even further."

Amara gestured, and the icy walls shimmered to life, revealing more scenes from Antarctica's distant past. This time, the images weren't of grand cities or alien ships but smaller, scattered communities. "Not all who lived here sought grandeur," she explained. "Many civilizations thrived in harmony with the land, leaving behind little more than echoes in the ice." We watched as primitive settlements took shape—small clusters of homes built from natural materials, their inhabitants dressed in furs and leathers. They lived by hunting the abundant wildlife and harvesting plants that thrived during the periodic thaws. "These people understood the cycles of the Ice," Amara said. "They knew when to retreat and when to return, adapting their lives to the rhythms of the land. While they left no monuments, their knowledge of survival was unparalleled." Harrison leaned forward, fascinated. "Why don't we know about them? Wouldn't there be traces of their existence?" Amara smiled faintly. "The Ice is both a preserver and an eraser. What it buries, it protects, but it also conceals. Only those who truly seek will find what lies beneath."

The images shifted to a more recent era—if thousands of years could be considered recent. We saw the early Guardians, a group of beings who looked strikingly similar to the Guardians we knew but with subtle differences. Their robes were simpler, their demeanor less refined. "Our ancestors," Amara said, her voice tinged with pride. "They were chosen not by bloodline but by merit, selected from the surviving civilizations to steward this land." The vision showed these proto-Guardians learning from the remnants of the alien technology, deciphering its secrets, and using it to stabilize the volatile environment. They created the first iterations of the Ice Cities, blending advanced technology with natural elements. "It was not an easy path," Amara continued. "There were conflicts, even among the Guardians. Some believed that humanity should inherit this knowledge, while others argued for secrecy."

Then the image of a fierce debate filled the icy wall. One faction of Guardians gestured passionately, while the other stood resolute, their faces cold and unyielding. "In the end, the decision was made to preserve the knowledge and guide humanity indirectly," Amara said. "But not all agreed. Some left, taking what they had learned with them." I felt a chill, and it wasn't from the cold air. "What happened to the ones who left?" I asked. "They disappeared into the Ice," Amara said simply. "Perhaps they perished, or perhaps they found something else. Their fate remains a mystery." "Larry This could be the ancient Elorans" Angel whispered to me.

Then the next scenes were more familiar—images of explorers, scientific expeditions, and the signing of the Antarctic Treaty. But Amara added layers of meaning to what we thought we knew. "The treaty was not merely a human initiative," she said. "We influenced its creation, ensuring that Antarctica would remain a place of peace and discovery." The Guardians appeared in the images, subtly guiding diplomats and scientists. It was clear they had been orchestrating events from behind the scenes, ensuring that humanity's approach to this land remained cautious and respectful. "Why allow exploration at all?" Sarah asked. "Wouldn't it be safer to keep everyone out?" Amara's expression softened. "Knowledge must be earned, not given. Humanity's curiosity is its greatest strength and its greatest weakness. By allowing exploration, we give you the chance to prove yourselves worthy."

Then the final part of their account delved into something entirely new: the Ice itself. Amara gestured, and the walls displayed intricate crystalline patterns, each one unique and mesmerizing. "The Ice is not merely frozen water," she said. "It is a living entity, a repository of memories and energy. Every event that has transpired here is etched into its structure." We saw visions of the Ice glowing faintly, reacting to the presence of people. It seemed almost sentient, shifting and reshaping itself in response to their movements. "It is both a guardian and a gatekeeper," Amara continued. "It protects what lies beneath but also offers glimpses to those who seek." Angel's eyes widened. "Is that why the Ice seemed to respond to us during the storm?" "Yes," Amara said. "It sensed your determination and your bond. The Ice can be a formidable ally—or an implacable foe."

So as the images faded, Amara's tone grew grave. "You now know more than most who have ever set foot on this land. But with knowledge comes responsibility." She stepped closer, her piercing gaze meeting each of ours in turn. "There are forces at work beyond your understanding. If you are not careful, the Ice will consume you as it has consumed so many before." I felt a shiver run down my spine. The weight of her words was undeniable. And as we left the chamber, Angel and I walked in silence, each lost in our thoughts. Finally, she spoke. "Do you think we're ready for what's coming?" I glanced at her, seeing the strength in her eyes despite the uncertainty in her voice. "I don't know," I admitted. "But I do know one thing: we don't face it alone."

(New Truths for Elora)

On the next day the journey back to Elora felt different this time. It wasn't the thrill of discovery or the weight of the unknown propelling us forward. It was purpose—a shared understanding that what we carried wasn't just information, but a piece of a much larger truth. Angel walked beside me, her face a mixture of determination and trepidation. The Guardians had approved her decision to return to Elora and share what we had learned, but even they couldn't predict how her people would react. "I'm not sure they'll believe me," Angel confessed, her voice barely hearable over the crunch of the snow beneath our boots. "They'll believe you," I said, squeezing her hand gently. "You're their connection to the outside world. If anyone can bridge this gap, it's you." She nodded, though her grip on my hand tightened. Ahead of us, the research team trudged silently, their expressions a mix of awe and exhaustion. The icy wilderness stretched endlessly in all directions, the harsh landscape was a reminder of the challenges we had faced and those still ahead.

Now the journey to Elora took several days, each one marked by a sense of anticipation that hung heavy in the frigid air. And as we approached the hidden city, the stark contrast between the barren ice and the vibrant glow of Elora's towers became more pronounced. Angel's pace quickened as we drew nearer, her steps lighter, more assured. The rest of us, however, hesitated. For all its beauty, Elora was still an enigma—a place that defied the rules of nature and challenged our understanding of the world. So when we finally reached the gates, a group of Eloran guards greeted us, their expressions stoic but not unkind. Angel stepped forward, speaking in their language with a fluidity that always amazed me. After a brief exchange, they gestured for us to follow.

And inside the city, we were led directly to the central hall, where the Eloran council awaited. The chamber was as grand as I remembered, its crystalline walls shimmering with an inner light that seemed to pulse in time with the energy of the city itself. Angel stood before the council, her posture poised but her hands trembling slightly. I stood just behind her, offering silent support. "Esteemed council," she began, her voice steady despite the tension in the room. "I have returned with knowledge that must be shared—knowledge that changes everything we thought we knew about our past." The council members exchanged glances, their expressions unreadable. Finally, the eldest of them, a woman named Lysera, spoke. "You have always been a voice for seeking the truth, Angel. But truths are not always easy to hear. Speak, and we will listen."

Angel recounted everything we had learned, from the alien origins of the Ice Cities to the forgotten civilizations that had thrived before Elora. Her words were measured and deliberate, each one carrying the weight of the history she sought to convey. The council listened intently, their expressions growing more serious as she delved into the details. When she spoke of the Guardians' revelations about Antarctica's creation and the civilizations that had risen and fallen over millennia's, a ripple of shock passed through the chamber. "You mean to say," Lysera interrupted, "that Elora is not the pinnacle of creation, but merely one chapter in a much longer story?" "Yes," Angel said firmly. "We are not the first, nor will we be the last. The Ice has seen more than we can imagine. To deny this truth is to deny our place in the greater history of this land."

The room erupted in murmurs, some council members nodding in agreement while others exchanged skeptical glances. One man, his voice sharp with disbelief, stood abruptly. "This is preposterous," he said. "Our ancestors created this city with their wisdom and strength. To suggest otherwise is an insult to their memory." Angel didn't falter. "It is not an insult to acknowledge the truth. Our ancestors were remarkable, but they were not alone. Their achievements do not diminish because others came before them." The man sat back down, though his scowl remained. Lysera raised a hand, silencing the room. "Angel speaks with conviction," she said. "But conviction alone is not proof. Do you have evidence to support these claims?" Angel turned to me, and I stepped forward, presenting a data pad filled with images and recordings from our expeditions. I explained the artifacts we had found, the records left by the Guardians, and the ancient city that even Elora's people hadn't known existed. "This is more than just theory," I said. "It's a tapestry of facts woven together over millennia's. The truth is undeniable."

The council studied the data in silence, their expressions shifting from skepticism to contemplation. Then finally, Lysera spoke again. "This changes much," she said. "But change is not to be feared. If what you say is true, then we must reconsider our place in the world—not as isolated beings, but as part of a much larger whole." Angel exhaled softly, relief evident on her face. But Lysera's gaze hardened as she turned to the rest of the team. "And what do you seek in return for sharing this knowledge?" "Nothing," I said quickly. "We came here to learn, not to take. All we ask is that you allow Angel the freedom to decide how best to bridge the gap between your people and ours." Lysera studied me for a long moment before nodding. "Very well. But know this: knowledge is a powerful tool, and its misuse can bring great harm. Use it wisely."

So as we left the chamber, Angel turned to me, her eyes shining with gratitude. "I didn't think they'd listen," she admitted. "They listened because you spoke from the heart," I said. "You're the bridge between two worlds, Angel. Never forget that." She smiled, leaning her head against my shoulder as we walked back to our quarters. The weight of what we had accomplished was heavy, but so was the hope it carried. For the first time, it felt like the barriers between Earth and Elora might truly begin to dissolve—not with force or fear, but with understanding.

So on the next day we went to the Eloran amphitheater, a breathtaking construct of crystalline walls and cascading light and it was also the 2nd location where Angel would speak to another group of her people, and it was filled to capacity. And for the first time since our arrival, the people of Elora had gathered in masse, their curiosity piqued by Angel's bold decision to reveal the truths we had uncovered. But her people trusted her—adored her even—but this was uncharted territory. She wasn't merely sharing stories; she was dismantling centuries of perceived history. But I stood to the side, partially hidden by a pillar of shimmering quartz, watching her prepare to speak. Her radiant presence was both calming and commanding. I could see the tension in her shoulders, the way she gripped the ancient scroll we'd recovered as if it were both a shield and a weapon. This wasn't just about recounting history; it was about reshaping their identity. "You've got this," I whispered to her as she passed me on her way to the center platform. She gave a small, grateful smile, and then she was there, standing before a sea of expectant faces.

"My friends, my family," Angel began, her voice clear and steady despite the weight of the moment. "For as long as we can remember, we have believed that Elora is the pinnacle of existence—our people, the culmination of what the Ice could nurture. But what if I told you that this isn't the whole story? What if I told you we are part of something much greater?" A murmur rippled through the crowd, a mix of intrigue and unease. Angel held up the scroll, the light catching its intricate symbols. "This," she said, "is a fragment of the Ice Chronicles, a record that predates Elora itself. It tells of civilizations that thrived long before ours, stretching back to the very creation of this land." She unrolled the scroll carefully, the ancient material glowing faintly in the ambient light. "These chronicles speak of the Guardians, the keepers of this land, and their role in preserving its secrets. They tell of a time when Antarctica wasn't just ice but a lush, thriving land, teeming with life."

And as Angel delved deeper into the Chronicles, she recounted the rise and fall of ancient civilizations—the ones who had walked these lands before the Ice claimed them. She spoke of their advancements, their struggles, and their eventual demise, painting a picture of a world that felt both foreign and eerily familiar. "They were not so different from us," she said, her voice tinged with sorrow. "They sought knowledge, built cities, and dreamed of a future brighter than their past. But they failed to understand the balance of this land, and the Ice became their undoing." A holographic projection illuminated behind her, showcasing the artifacts and inscriptions we had uncovered. The audience gasped at the sight of structures that bore striking similarities to Eloran architecture, proof that their ancestors had not been the first to master such designs.

"What does this mean for us?" one man in the crowd called out, his tone skeptical. "Are you saying we are merely imitators, living in the shadow of those who came before?" Angel shook her head. "No, it means we are inheritors of their legacy. We are the continuation of a story that spans millennia's. And their achievements do not diminish ours; they enrich them. But to honor that legacy, we must acknowledge the full truth of who we are and where we come from." Then the crowd buzzed with conversation, and I could see doubt and wonder mingling in their faces. Then Angel turned slightly, meeting my gaze, and I nodded encouragingly.

"There is more," Angel continued, raising her hands to quiet the crowd. "The Ice is not just a barrier—it is a bridge. Beyond it lies another world, one that we have kept ourselves separate from for too long." This revelation caused an uproar. Voices clashed, some demanding more information, others expressing disbelief. But Angel waited patiently for the noise to die down before continuing. "I have seen this other world with my own eyes," she said, her voice rising above the din. "I have walked among its people, learned of their history, and shared in their struggles. They are not our enemies. They are our kin, separated by time and circumstance but bound by the same spark of life." She gestured toward me, and I stepped forward, feeling the weight of countless eyes on me. "This is Larry Bridge," she said. "He is from that world—a world we once thought unreachable. He and his people carry knowledge that complements our own. And together, we can forge a future built on a mutual understanding."

Then the amphitheater erupted once more, the crowd splitting into factions. Some applauded, their faces lit with hope, while others shook their heads, their expressions dark with distrust. "This is madness," one elder declared, rising to his feet. "We cannot trust these outsiders. They will bring chaos to our way of life!" Angel's gaze hardened, and she stepped forward. "Change is always met with resistance," she said firmly. "But fear should not dictate our actions. If we are to thrive, we must embrace the truth and the opportunities it brings." Her words carried a conviction that silenced even the harshest critics. Slowly, the crowd began to calm, and their murmurs gave way to a thoughtful silence.

And after the assembly dispersed, Angel and I retreated to a quiet corner of the city. She leaned against me, exhaustion etched into her features. "You were incredible," I told her, brushing a strand of hair from her face. "I don't know if it was enough," she admitted. "But at least the seed has been planted." "It's more than enough," I assured her. "You've given them a chance to see the bigger picture and the rest will come in time." She smiled faintly, her resolve returning. "The Ice has kept its secrets for too long. It's time for us to be more than its prisoners."

(The Ancient Remnants)

The next day icy winds whistled through the jagged cliffs as we trudged toward the ancient city we had first stumbled upon weeks ago. Snow crunched beneath our boots, and the cold bit at our exposed skin despite our heavy gear. There was a different energy in the air this time—a palpable tension mixed with curiosity. For weeks, the city had lingered in the back of our minds, a mystery begging to be unraveled. Angel walked beside me, her steps light despite the treacherous terrain. The way her golden hair shimmered under the weak sunlight was a stark contrast to the desolation surrounding us. And behind us, the rest of the team carried equipment, their chatter minimal as we pressed forward. "Do you think we'll find anything new?" Angel asked, her voice soft yet steady. "I don't know," I admitted, gripping my walking stick tighter. "But something tells me the city isn't done with us yet."

So as we approached the outskirts of the ancient city, the towering structures loomed larger, their frost-covered facades etched with symbols that seemed almost alive in the diffused light and the air grew heavier, not just with the cold, but with a sense of foreboding. The Guardians who accompanied us exchanged uneasy glances, their usual stoicism shaken. Even Angel seemed more subdued, her gaze fixed on the massive archway that marked the city's entrance. "It feels different," Dr. Alan Harrison muttered, breaking the silence. "Like the place is... watching us." I didn't respond, but I couldn't shake the same feeling. The city, with its intricate carvings and sprawling courtyards, felt less abandoned this time—more aware.

So as we ventured deeper into the city, our flashlights slicing through the dimness. The temperature seemed to drop the farther we went, and our breaths visible in the freezing air. Then suddenly, a faint, flickering light caught our attention. "Do you see that?" Angel whispered, clutching my arm. I nodded, signaling the group to move quietly. The light was coming from a structure near the city's center, the one we hadn't explored during our previous visit. Its ornate design suggested it was once a place of great importance—a temple, perhaps, or a palace. So as we approached, the light grew steadier, revealing a doorway partially blocked by debris. Angel and I squeezed through the narrow opening first, then the rest of the team following close behind.

And inside, the air was warmer, almost suffocating. But the source of the light was an ancient, crystalline structure in the center of the room, glowing faintly with an otherworldly hue. But it wasn't the light that made us gasp—it was the figures huddled near it. There were five of them, their forms thin and frail, their skin a pale, almost translucent hue. And they looked human, but there was something... other about them. Their eyes, large and luminous, seemed to glow faintly in the dim light. Then one of them stood as we entered, and their movements slow and deliberate. Then they spoke in a language none of us understood, and their voice melodic yet haunting. Angel stepped forward, her expression was a mix of shock and empathy. "They're... alive," she whispered. Dr. Alan Harrison was already reaching for his translator device, but the being raised a hand, stopping him. Instead, they placed a hand on the crystalline structure, and suddenly, a wave of warmth and clarity washed over us. "We have waited," the being said, their voice now understandable. "For so long, we have waited."

Then the survivors, as we came to learn, were remnants of an ancient civilization predating even Elora. They had once thrived here, masters of the Ice and its secrets. But a cataclysmic event—one they referred to as "The Great Freeze"—had decimated their people, forcing them into the depths of the city. Then one of the ancient people spoke again "For centuries, we have endured," said the leader, who called themselves Kaelith. "The Ice is relentless, but we adapted. Our bodies changed to survive in its embrace, but we are no longer what we once were." Their story was heartbreaking, a testament to resilience in the face of unimaginable odds. Yet, it was clear that they were nearing the end of their struggle. Their supplies were dwindling, and their numbers had dwindled even further.

"We can't just leave them here," Angel said as we regrouped outside the structure. Her eyes were filled with determination, her hands gripping mine tightly. "They need our help." "She's right," Dr. Alan Harrison agreed. "But how do we even begin to help them? They've been surviving here for centuries under conditions we can barely endure for a few hours." Then the Guardians, who had remained silent until now, stepped forward. "There is a way," one of them said, their voice grave. "But it will require great sacrifice. To restore balance, the city must be reawakened." "What does that mean?" I asked, my heart sinking at the weight of their words. "It means returning the city to its former glory," the Guardian replied. "The survivors can be saved, but it will not be easy. The Ice resists change, and it will fight back."

So as we prepared to leave the city, our minds heavy with the revelations and the weight of the task ahead, I couldn't help but glance back at Kaelith and their people. Despite their frailty, there was a quiet strength in their eyes—a glimmer of hope that had refused to be extinguished. "We'll come back," I promised them, my voice firm. "We'll find a way to help." Kaelith nodded, their expression unreadable. "The Ice holds many secrets," they said. "But it also holds the key to our salvation. Trust in its wisdom, and you will find the way." And as we made our way back to camp, I felt a renewed sense of purpose. The journey ahead would be perilous, but it wasn't just about discovery anymore—it was about survival, about ensuring that the stories of these people, and their incredible resilience, would not be lost to the Ice.

So it began subtly, almost imperceptibly. A soft hum vibrated through the frozen air, resonating deep within the ancient structures. Standing at the edge of the city's central plaza, Then I felt it in my chest first—a faint but steady rhythm, like a heartbeat. And it wasn't just sound; it was life, slowly reemerging from the slumber of countless centuries. Then the crystalline obelisks scattered throughout the city shimmered faintly under the icy sunlight. And Angel stood beside me, her eyes wide with wonder, and her hand clasped tightly in mine and behind us, the team and the Guardians worked tirelessly, activating a sequence of devices we could barely comprehend. "This is it," Dr. Alan Harrison said, his voice hushed as he adjusted a control panel covered in glowing symbols. "The first stage of reawakening."

The Guardians had given us specific instructions, their voices heavy with the weight of ancient knowledge. The city, they explained, was not just a collection of structures but a living entity, interconnected through a network of crystalline energy conduits buried beneath the ice. "Awakening the city will require harmony," one of the Guardians had told us the night before. "The energy must flow without obstruction, and the Ice must accept its return." Then for days, we worked tirelessly, guided by the Guardians. And we cleared debris from key sites, repaired damaged conduits, and calibrated ancient mechanisms that responded to touch as though they recognized us. And Angel proved invaluable during this process, her innate understanding of the city's architecture surpassing even the Guardians'. "This place feels alive," she had said during one late-night session, her voice tinged with awe. "Like it remembers what it used to be and wants to be whole again."

Then when the moment finally arrived, it was both exhilarating and terrifying. And the Guardians instructed us to gather in the central plaza, where the largest crystalline obelisk towered over the city. It was here that the heart of the city resided, and they explained—a core of energy that had been dormant for millennia's. Then Angel and I stood close together as the Guardians activated the obelisk. And as a surge of light coursed through the structure, illuminating the intricate carvings etched into its surface. Then the hum grew louder, resonating with a pitch that seemed to echo through the depths of the Ice itself. Then suddenly, beams of light shot out from the obelisk, connecting with smaller crystals scattered across the city. Then the conduits beneath our feet began to glow, tracing a luminous network that pulsed with energy. And the entire city seemed to come alive before our eyes, its dormant beauty revealed in breathtaking detail.

"It's... incredible," Angel whispered, her voice trembling with emotion. I could only nod, overwhelmed by the sheer majesty of what we were witnessing. The city, once cloaked in frost and shadow, now radiated a warm, golden light. Its towers gleamed like polished glass, and its streets, once cracked and uneven, smoothed themselves as if healing from centuries of decay. The survivors, led by Kaelith, emerged from their shelter to witness the transformation. Their pale, fragile forms seemed to regain some vitality under the city's light. They knelt near the central obelisk, their hands outstretched as if to embrace the energy coursing through their home. "This is what we have waited for," Kaelith said, their voice steady but filled with awe. "Our city, our lifeblood, restored."

And despite the awe-inspiring sight, the reawakening was not without its challenges. The Ice, resistant to change, seemed to fight back. Cracks formed in the streets as pockets of frost expanded beneath the surface. "We're destabilizing the area," Dr. Alan Harrison warned, his voice urgent as he monitored a handheld device. "The Ice isn't just going to let this happen without a fight." The Guardians moved swiftly, using their advanced technology to stabilize the conduits and contain the energy flow. Angel joined them, her instincts proving invaluable once again. "Larry," she called out, her voice sharp with focus. "Help me with this panel. If we can redirect the flow here, it might prevent a collapse." I rushed to her side, following her instructions as best as I could. Sweat dripped down my face despite the freezing air, but together, we managed to stabilize the system.

Then when the final adjustments were made, the city's transformation reached its climax. The light from the obelisk intensified, shooting into the sky like a beacon. Then the air grew warmer, the frost retreating from the buildings and revealing intricate mosaics and carvings hidden beneath. The Guardians stood in silent reverence, their faces illuminated by the glow. Then the survivors, now standing tall and proud, began to chant in their ancient language, their voices harmonizing with the hum of the city. Then Angel turned to me, her eyes shining with tears. "We did it, Larry," she said, her voice trembling. "We brought it back." I pulled her into an embrace, overwhelmed by the magnitude of what we had accomplished. And for the first time since we'd arrived in this frozen wasteland, I felt a deep, unshakable hope. Then as the light settled into a steady glow, the city's transformation became complete. It was no longer a ruin but a thriving, living monument to the past. The Guardians explained that the city's energy would sustain the survivors and the Ice itself, creating a delicate balance that would ensure its longevity.

"This is only the beginning," Kaelith said. "The city's reawakening is not just for us but for all who dwell beyond the Ice." I nodded, understanding the weight of their words. This wasn't just a victory for the survivors or the Guardians—it was a victory for humanity, a reminder of what we could achieve when we worked together. And as we prepared to leave the plaza, Then I took one last look at the glowing city, and its beauty etched into my memory forever. This place, this moment, was a testament to resilience, to hope, and to the enduring spirit of those who refused to be forgotten.

(The Journey Back)

In the following days the decision to leave the Ancient City weighed heavily on all of us. After days of deliberation, Angel, the team, and I finally agreed that it was time to return to the research station. The city was alive now, thriving under the guardianship of its original inhabitants and the newly awakened energy conduits. Yet, despite its progress, lingering concerns about the instability of the Ice and the unknown implications of our presence made us feel that our work there was complete—for now. We set out at dawn, the crystalline city gleaming behind us as we trudged through the snow-laden terrain. A quiet solemnity had settled over the group, a mixture of accomplishment and the uncertainty of what lay ahead. I couldn't help but glance back at Angel, her face illuminated by the early sunlight but she looked torn, her attachment to both her homeland and her desire to see the rest of the world palpable in her expression.

"You okay?" I asked her as we paused for a moment to adjust our gear. She gave me a small, wistful smile. "I'm fine, Larry. Just... wondering if we're making the right decision." "We'll come back," I assured her, gripping her hand briefly. "This isn't goodbye." She nodded, though her eyes lingered on the city's distant spires before she turned back toward the horizon. Then the first few days of our journey started and they were uneventful, though exhausting. The icy wilderness stretched endlessly in every direction, an unforgiving expanse of white that seemed to swallow the horizon. The sleds we'd packed with supplies creaked under their weight, and the biting wind found every exposed inch of skin, no matter how tightly we bundled ourselves. The Guardians had given us detailed maps and guidance for navigating the terrain, but even their knowledge couldn't fully account for the unpredictability of the Ice, and later that day Dr. Alan Harrison and Kaelith often huddled over the maps during our brief breaks, debating the best routes and adjusting our course as necessary and Angel stayed close to me throughout the journey, her presence a constant comfort in the desolate landscape. As we spoke often, sharing stories about our lives before this expedition, imagining what our future together might hold.

And it was on the fourth day that the weather began to change. The first signs were subtle—a drop in temperature, a sudden stillness in the air—but they were enough to make the Guardians uneasy. "We need to move quickly," one of them warned. "The Ice is restless." Then by the fifth day, the sky had darkened, heavy clouds rolling in like a tidal wave. Snow began to fall, light at first but growing steadily heavier. The wind picked up, howling across the plains and whipping the snow into blinding swirls. "Looks like we're in for a storm," Dr.

Alan Harrison muttered, pulling his scarf tighter around his face. I exchanged a worried glance with Angel. We both knew what a blizzard could mean out here—zero visibility, plummeting temperatures, and a very real risk of losing our way.

And by the time night fell, the storm was in full force. Snow pelted us relentlessly, stinging our faces and piling up around our legs as we struggled to set up a makeshift camp. The sleds were barely visible through the swirling snow, and our voices were nearly drowned out by the wind. "Everyone, stick together!" Dr. Alan Harrison shouted. "We'll dig in here for the night!" We worked quickly, carving out a sheltered space in the snow and erecting our tents as best as we could. The Guardians used their technology to create a temporary heat source, which provided some relief from the biting cold.

Then inside the tent, Angel and I huddled together, our breath visible in the dim light and her hands were ice-cold despite her gloves, and I wrapped my arms around her, trying to share whatever warmth I could. "This storm," she murmured, her voice muffled against my shoulder. "It feels... unnatural." I didn't disagree. There was an intensity to it, a fury that seemed almost deliberate.

Then when morning came, the blizzard showed no signs of letting up. The wind continued to howl, and the snowdrifts around our camp had grown alarmingly high. Visibility was still near zero, and even the Guardians seemed at a loss for how to proceed. "We can't stay here indefinitely," Kaelith said during a tense meeting in one of the larger tents. "But moving in these conditions could be even more dangerous." "Do we have enough supplies to wait it out?" I asked, glancing at the sleds where our food and equipment were stored. "Barely," Dr. Harrison replied grimly. "If this storm doesn't let up soon, we're going to have to make a run for it." And the longer we remained trapped, the more the tension within the group grew. Exhaustion and fear began to take their toll, fraying tempers and making even small disagreements feel monumental. Angel and I did our best to keep our spirits up, sharing stories and encouraging the others to stay hopeful, but it was clear that everyone was struggling. At night, and the storm seemed to grow even louder, and the wind battering the tents and shaking their fragile frames. Sleep was nearly impossible, and I found myself lying awake, staring at the faint glow of our heat source and worrying about what would happen if we couldn't find a way out.

But on the seventh day, there was a brief lull in the storm. The wind eased slightly, and the snow fell less heavily, allowing us a small window of opportunity. "This might be our chance," Kaelith said, their voice cautious but determined. "If we move quickly, we might be able to make some progress before the storm picks up again." We packed up the camp as quickly as we could, bracing ourselves for the treacherous journey ahead. The Guardians led the way, their knowledge of the terrain our best hope of finding a safe route.

So as we trudged through the snow, I kept a firm grip on Angel's hand, determined not to let anything separate us. Despite the danger, there was a strange sense of resolve among the group. But we had survived so much already—surely, we could survive this too. And by the time we thought we had reached the storm's peak, it became clear we had been wrong. The blizzard roared with an unrelenting fury, a symphony of chaos that drowned out even our thoughts. And snow fell so densely it felt like the very sky was collapsing around us, and the wind cut through our layers of clothing as if they weren't even there.

And each step felt like a battle against an invisible enemy. And the sleds were nearly buried beneath the accumulating drifts, and the biting cold made every movement painful and so much that I couldn't even feel my face anymore, and the distant ache in my fingers told me frostbite might not be far off if we didn't find better shelter soon. "Keep moving!" Kaelith yelled from somewhere ahead, their voice barely hearable over the storm's deafening howl. Then I tightened my grip on Angel's hand, my fingers numb but unwilling to let go. Then she stumbled slightly, and I pulled her upright, her eyes meeting mine briefly through the frosted goggles. "I'm okay," she assured me, though her voice trembled with exhaustion. "You're not okay," I said, leaning closer so she could hear me. "None of us are." Her lips quirked into a faint, fleeting smile. "But we're still alive."

Then it seemed like the landscape had become an endless, featureless void. The horizon was gone, swallowed by the storm, and even the Guardians seemed unsure of our location. The maps they carried were useless now—there were no landmarks, no way to orient ourselves in the blinding white chaos. "We need to stop," Dr. Harrison shouted, his voice tinged with panic. "If we keep going like this, we're going to lose someone." "And if we stop, we freeze," Kaelith countered, their tone grim. "We're already freezing!" Harrison snapped. "Enough!" I yelled, cutting through their argument. "We're all in this together. If we fall apart now, we're finished." Their faces softened slightly, though the tension between them lingered.

Then later that day the Guardians suggested a desperate plan: using their advanced tech to create a new temporary heat bubble that could sustain us while we waited out the worst of the storm. It wasn't a perfect solution—and the tech had limits, and also the energy reserves were finite—but it was better than nothing. So we clustered together as the Guardians activated the device. A faint hum emerged, and a shimmering dome of light appeared around us, pushing back the snow and providing a small pocket of warmth. It wasn't much, but it was enough to stave off the worst of the cold for now. And inside the bubble, the mood was somber. Angel leaned against me, her breathing shallow, and I wrapped my arm around her, trying to lend her my strength. "This isn't natural," she murmured. "The storm... it's like it's alive." I didn't know how to respond but she wasn't wrong. There was something almost sentient about the storm's ferocity, as if it were deliberately trying to drive us back—or destroy us entirely.

Then as time passed the bubble held for hours, but the storm showed no signs of abating. Snow piled up around us, pressing against the dome and making it feel like we were trapped inside a shrinking cage. Supplies were running low, and the cold seeped into our bones despite the heat source. "This can't go on much longer," Kaelith admitted, but their normally stoic demeanor cracking. "The tech won't hold up if the storm intensifies again." "What do we do?" Dr. Harrison asked but Kaelith didn't answer, their gaze fixed on the swirling snow beyond the dome.

Then just when it seemed like all hope was lost, there was a sudden break in the wind. It was brief—only a few minutes—but it was enough for the Guardians to scan the area and identify a potential route to higher ground. "If we can make it there, we might find better shelter," one of them said. "It's a risk," I said, glancing at Angel. She looked exhausted but nodded in agreement. "We don't have a choice," she said. So we packed up as quickly as possible, and the group moving with a sense of urgency despite the cold sapping our strength. Then the break in the storm didn't last, and as we trudged through the snow once more, the blizzard seemed to redouble its efforts, battering us with icy fury. And by the time we reached the base of the ridge, several of us were on the verge of collapse. The climb was treacherous, the snow slick and unstable, but the thought of better shelter kept us going. "Just a little further," I urged Angel, though my own legs felt like they might give out at any moment. She nodded, her determination as fierce as ever. Together, we pushed on, the group slowly but steadily making its way upward. And when we finally reached the plateau, the sight that greeted us was almost surreal. The snow had eased slightly, revealing a jagged outcrop of Ice that formed a natural barrier against the wind. It wasn't perfect, but it was the best shelter we'd seen in days.

(Shadowed Horizons)

So as time passed I'd thought the blizzard was the worst it could get. I thought the unrelenting cold, the biting wind, and the endless, blinding snow were nature's ultimate cruelty. But nature, it seemed, had nothing to do with what came next. It started with the shadows. At first, they were nothing more than faint impressions in the swirling snow—fleeting, indistinct shapes that could have been tricks of the light or exhaustion playing games with our minds. But they grew bolder. "Did you see that?" Angel asked, her voice trembling as she tightened her grip on my arm. "See what?" I replied, though I already knew what she was talking about. "That... thing," she said, her eyes darting into the storm. "Something's out there." Then Kaelith, who had been scouting ahead, turned back with a grim expression. "We're being followed," he said, with his voice calm but carrying an unmistakable edge of urgency.

Then the first clear glimpse of them froze us all in place. Towering forms emerged from the snow, their outlines barely visible against the white fury of the storm. They moved with an unnatural grace, their massive, shadowed bodies blending seamlessly with the blizzard, as if they were part of it. "What the hell are those?" Dr. Harrison whispered, with his voice barely heard over the wind. "Adversaries," Kaelith said darkly. "They're no longer just influences. They've taken form." The shadows loomed closer, their indistinct shapes resolving into grotesque figures that defied logic. They had no defined faces, just swirling voids where eyes and mouths might have been, and their massive limbs seemed to stretch and contract unnaturally as they moved. "Run!" Kaelith shouted.

And we didn't need to be told twice then the team broke into a desperate sprint, the snow slowing our progress as the shadowed figures closed in. Then their movements were impossibly fast, like predators toying with their prey. And Angel clung to my hand, her breathing ragged as we pushed forward. I could hear the pounding of my own heartbeat over the storm, and every instinct screaming at me to keep moving, to not look back. But I did. And one of the figures reached out, its massive hand-like shadow swiping through the snow but it narrowly missed Kaelith, who darted to the side with a precision that seemed almost superhuman. "They're herding us!" Kaelith yelled. "What?" I shouted back. "They're not trying to kill us—yet. They're driving us somewhere!"

So as we stumbled into a narrow ravine, its steep walls providing some shelter from the worst of the wind but leaving us trapped and the adversaries didn't hesitate. They followed us in, their forms growing larger and more defined as they approached. "We can't outrun them!" Dr. Harrison gasped, his face pale with terror then Kaelith stopped abruptly, turning to face the oncoming shadows. "Keep going," they ordered, their tone brooking no argument. "What are you doing?" Angel demanded. "Buying you time," Kaelith said simply, their hand reaching for a device strapped to their belt. "No!" I shouted, but it was too late. Kaelith activated the device, a blinding burst of light erupting from it. Then the shadows recoiled, their forms flickering and distorting as if the light were tearing them apart. "Go!" Kaelith yelled, their voice barely hearable over the deafening hum of the device.

And as we ran, guilt and fear mixing in my chest as Kaelith's figure disappeared behind us. The light from their device faded quickly, and I didn't dare think about what might have happened to them. Then the ravine opened up into a frozen plain, and the blizzard still raging but the adversaries momentarily out of sight. So we collapsed into a huddle, gasping for breath, our bodies trembling from exhaustion and cold. "Kaelith..." Angel began, her voice breaking. "They'll be fine," I said, though I didn't believe my own words. "They're strong. They'll find us again." The others didn't respond, their faces etched with exhaustion and despair. And for a brief moment, the storm seemed to ease, and we could see the faint outlines of what looked like a cave in the distance. "Shelter," Angel said, with her voice barely above a whisper. "It's our best chance," I agreed. So we forced ourselves to our feet, every step toward the cave feeling like an eternity. And the shadows still didn't reappear, but their presence lingered in the back of my mind, an oppressive weight that refused to lift. Then when we finally reached the cave, we collapsed inside, the relative calm of the interior a stark contrast to the chaos outside. "They're not done with us," Angel said quietly, as her gaze fixed on the entrance. "No," I agreed, wrapping my arm around her. "But we're not done fighting, either."

Then the calm after the storm was deceptive and for a brief moment, the howling wind outside the cave seemed to relent, giving us the illusion of safety. Inside, our breaths came heavy, and the only sound besides the occasional crack of shifting ice. Angel leaned against me, her body trembling—not just from the cold, but from fear. "Do you think they're gone?" Dr. Harrison asked, with his voice low. "No," Kaelith said flatly, their eyes fixed on the cave's entrance. They had rejoined us not long after the blinding light had forced the shadows back, battered but alive. "They're regrouping."

Then as if on cue, a deep, resonating sound echoed through the blizzard. It wasn't natural, more like a low, guttural hum that seemed to vibrate through the ice itself. "They're coming," Angel whispered, clutching my arm tightly. Then the first sign of their reappearance was the darkness. Not the kind caused by the absence of light, but a suffocating, unnatural blackness that crept into the edges of the cave like living smoke. "We need to move," Kaelith said. "Move where?" Dr.

Harrison snapped. "We're in the middle of nowhere!" Then before anyone could respond, the cave's entrance erupted in chaos and the shadows from before materialized, no longer indistinct forms but massive, towering figures with grotesque, writhing features. And their limbs stretched and coiled like smoke, but their movements were precise, purposeful. "Go!" Kaelith shouted, shoving us toward the back of the cave.

Then as we scrambled out into the storm, the brief shelter of the cave forgotten. And the blizzard had returned with a vengeance, snow whipping against our faces and reducing visibility to mere feet. And behind us, the adversaries pursued. Their shadowed forms cut through the snow effortlessly, their size and speed defying logic. And they didn't seem hindered by the storm; if anything, it seemed to bow to their presence. "They're gaining!" Dr. Harrison shouted, but his voice was barely hearable over the wind. "Head for the ridge!" Kaelith yelled, pointing to a jagged outline in the distance. "We can lose them in the ice fields!" Reaching the ridge was a trial in itself. And the snow was knee-deep in places, making every step a battle. Angel stayed close to me though, and her hand gripping mine tightly. "Don't let go," she said, with her voice trembling but determined. "I won't," I promised, though my own fear was threatening to overwhelm me.

Then we crested the ridge, only to find ourselves facing a labyrinth of towering ice formations. Massive spires and walls of translucent blue stretched in every direction, their surfaces glistening ominously in the storm's light. "This way!" Kaelith led us into the maze, their movements quick and deliberate despite the treacherous terrain. But the adversaries followed, their towering forms dwarfing the ice spires. And they moved with an eerie fluidity, slipping between the narrow passages as if the ice itself bent to accommodate them. Then one of them lunged forward, a massive arm-like appendage slamming into the ground mere inches from where Angel and I stood. The impact sent a tremor through the ice, knocking us off balance. "Keep moving!" Kaelith shouted, pulling us to our feet. Then as we zigzagged through the maze, the shadows always just a step behind. Their guttural hums filled the air, a sound that seemed to bypass my ears and settle directly in my chest.

Then at one point, the path narrowed to a single-file passage, forcing us to slow down. It was then that one of the adversaries struck. A tendril of shadow shot forward, wrapping around Harrison's leg and yanking him off his feet. "Help me!" he screamed, clawing at the ice. Kaelith didn't hesitate. Then he turned and activated another of his devices, and a pulse of light forcing the shadow to release its grip. Harrison scrambled to his feet, his face pale with terror, and we kept moving. Then finally, we emerged from the ice maze into a small, sheltered basin. Then the adversaries halted at the edge of the maze, and their forms writhing in frustration as if the ice itself had become a barrier. "They can't follow us here,"

Kaelith said, their breathing labored. "Why not?" Angel asked, her voice shaking. Kaelith didn't answer immediately then he simply stared at the adversaries, with his expression unreadable. "They're afraid of something," Kaelith said finally. "Something in this place."

Then as we collapsed into the basin, too exhausted to go any further. Angel leaned against me, her breathing heavy but steady. "What are they?" she asked softly. "Trouble," I said, trying to inject some humor into my tone. But it didn't work. "They're more than that," Kaelith said, his gaze still fixed on the adversaries. "They're ancient. Older than anything on this continent." Then as we sat in the relative calm of the basin, I couldn't help but feel the weight of everything we'd experienced. The adversaries weren't just a threat; they were a force of nature, a reminder that we were intruding on something far beyond our understanding. But as I looked at Angel, her face lit by the faint glow of the ice around us, I felt a renewed sense of purpose. "We'll get through this," I said, more to myself than anyone else. Angel nodded, her hand finding mine. "We have to."

(The Final Stand)

So as time passed the storm raged on and we prepared for what felt like the end and each of us had found a corner of the icy basin to brace ourselves against, weapons, tools, and what little courage we had left at the ready. But the adversaries hadn't crossed into the basin yet, but their ominous presence lingered just beyond the towering spires of ice and their guttural hums reverberated through the air, a chilling melody of malevolence. Then Angel sat beside me, her fingers entwined with mine. Her warmth was the only thing anchoring me in this frozen hellscape. "They're coming," she whispered, her voice steady despite the fear in her eyes. "I know," I said, squeezing her hand. I glanced around at the others—Kaelith standing firm with his advanced tech, Harrison and Sarah huddled together, visibly terrified but resolved. This was it. We all knew it. Kaelith broke the silence. "If we fail here, they won't stop. They'll consume everything—Elora, Earth, all of it. We can't let that happen." Their words hit me like a punch to the gut. Failure wasn't an option. So I looked at Angel, her golden and hair glowing faintly in the eerie light. Then she nodded as if reading my thoughts. "We'll fight," she said. "Together."

Then the adversaries emerged from the shadows, their forms no longer restrained by the edges of the basin. And they had grown even more massive, their smoky, shifting bodies solidifying into grotesque shapes—towering humanoid figures with elongated limbs and eyes like burning coals. And one of them let out a deafening roar, the sound reverberating through the ice and shaking the ground beneath us. They were here to end us. "Hold your ground!" Kaelith shouted, activating a shield device that created a shimmering barrier of light around us. The adversaries hesitated for a moment, their movements jerky and uncertain, but then they pressed forward.

Then the first adversary lunged at the barrier, its shadowy arm slamming against the light. Then the shield held, but only barely and the force of the impact sent a shockwave through the air, knocking us off balance. Kaelith retaliated with a pulse grenade, the burst of light momentarily scattering the adversary's form. "They're vulnerable to light!" they shouted. I grabbed a flare from our pack and ignited it, tossing it at the nearest shadow. It writhed and shrieked as the light burned through its form, but it wasn't enough to destroy it. "We need more!" Harrison yelled, frantically lighting another flare. Then Angel stood beside me, with her face pale but determined. "We have to do this together," she said, her voice firm.

Then as the battle raged, Angel and I found ourselves back-to-back, fending off the shadows with flares and anything else we could find. But no matter how many we repelled, more kept coming. "They're too strong!" Sarah screamed, her voice filled with despair. "No," Angel said, her voice cutting through the chaos. "They're not. Not if we stand together." She turned to me, her eyes glowing with an inner light I hadn't noticed before. "Larry, I believe in us. In this." Before I could respond, she kissed me. It was like the world stopped. The storm, the cold, the fear—all of it melted away in that moment. And then, the light came.

It started as a faint glow, emanating from where Angel and I stood. Then it grew brighter and brighter, until it engulfed the entire basin in a radiant, golden light. The adversaries froze, their forms quivering as if in pain. "What's happening?" Kaelith shouted, shielding their eyes. I didn't know how to explain it. All I knew was that the love I felt for Angel, the connection we shared, was creating something extraordinary—something the adversaries couldn't withstand. The light intensified, piercing through the shadows like a blade. One by one, the adversaries disintegrated, their forms unraveling into wisps of smoke that were carried away by the wind.

Then within minutes, it was over. The basin was silent, the storm suddenly calm. The adversaries were gone, their presence erased entirely. I looked at Angel, who was still glowing faintly. She smiled, her face filled with both relief and awe. "We did it," she said softly. Kaelith approached us, with his expression unreadable. "I don't know what that was," he said, "but it saved all of us. Thank you." "It wasn't just us," I said, looking around at the others. "We all played a part."

And as the sun began to rise over the horizon, casting its first rays of light across the ice, I felt a sense of peace I hadn't known in weeks. The fight was over. The adversaries were defeated. But I also knew this was just the beginning. And the bond between Angel and me had unlocked something powerful, something that could change the course of history—but not just for us, but for everyone. "We have a lot of work to do," Angel said, taking my hand. I nodded, smiling despite the exhaustion that weighed on me. "Yeah," I said. "But we'll do it together."

(A Hero's Return)

The next day I noticed the towering gates of Guardian City came into view as we trudged through the icy wilderness, the warmth of the golden lights spilling over the snow-covered ground a stark contrast to the cold and chaos we had just endured. Then Angel tightened her grip on my hand, her touch both comforting and grounding. And beside us, the rest of the team followed closely, their faces etched with exhaustion but also relief. We had survived the impossible, and now, it seemed, we were about to be recognized for it. Then the gates swung open with a low hum, revealing a city alive with anticipation. Guardians lined the streets, their ethereal forms shimmering under the pale sunlight. Their robes, a blend of silver and blue, flowed like water as they raised their arms in unison to greet us. A resounding cheer echoed through the city, the sound washing over us like a wave. "We weren't expecting this," Sarah muttered, her voice filled with awe. Kaelith chuckled, though his voice was weary. "The Guardians value acts of bravery and unity. What we did back there... it's something they'll never forget."

And as we entered the city, the Guardians began to sing. And their voices were unlike anything I had ever heard—soft, melodic, and layered with harmonies that seemed to resonate deep within my chest. And the streets were adorned with banners of light, their patterns shifting and changing as if alive. Angel looked up at me, her eyes sparkling with wonder. "This is incredible," she said. "It feels surreal," I replied, my gaze sweeping over the scene. "After everything we've been through, I didn't think I'd feel... hopeful again." Then the Guardians led us through the streets in a grand procession, and their movements graceful and deliberate. Then as we walked, I couldn't help but notice the respect in their eyes, and the way they bowed slightly as we passed and it was clear that what we had done—defeating the adversaries—had deeply impacted them.

Then our journey ended at the Hall of Light, a massive structure carved into the heart of the city. Its crystalline walls glowed with an inner luminescence, casting rainbow-like reflections that danced across the ground. The main chamber was even more breathtaking, with a vaulted ceiling that seemed to stretch endlessly upward and a circular platform at its center. Then the High Guardian, a figure taller and more radiant than the others, stepped forward. his voice, calm yet powerful, filled the chamber. "Larry Bridge, Angel, and the members of the Earth research team—your bravery has saved not only this city but the balance of the world itself. For that, we owe you a debt that can never be repaid." I felt a lump rise in my throat as the High Guardian extended his hands toward us. "Step forward, heroes." We approached the platform hesitantly, the weight of the moment sinking in. Angel glanced at me, her expression a mix of pride and humility. "You were right," she whispered. "We did this together." Then the High Guardian placed a glowing crystal in my hands, its warmth seeping into my skin. "This is the Light of Unity," they explained. "A symbol of the bond you share and the strength it has given all of us." And as I held the crystal, I felt a surge of energy, a reminder of the light Angel and I had unleashed during the battle. Then the crowd erupted into applause, and their cheers filling the chamber.

Then the ceremony gave way to a citywide celebration. Then as the Guardians prepared a feast in our honor, with tables stretching the length of the main square and dishes crafted from ingredients I couldn't begin to identify. The air was filled with laughter and music, a stark contrast to the somber days leading up to this moment. As Angel and I sat side by side, sharing a meal and a quiet smile. Around us, the team mingled with the Guardians, their earlier exhaustion replaced with a sense of belonging. Sarah raised a glass, her voice cutting through the chatter. "To Larry and Angel," she said, grinning. "Our unlikely heroes." "To all of us," I corrected, lifting my own glass. "None of this would have been possible without every single one of you."

And as the celebration ended, I found myself standing on one of the city's balconies, gazing out at the icy expanse beyond and Angel joined me, slipping her arm through mine. "What's on your mind?" she asked softly. "Everything," I admitted. "What we've been through, what we've discovered... It's overwhelming. But I feel like we're on the brink of something extraordinary." Then Angel smiled, resting her head on my shoulder. "We are," she said. "And we'll face it together." As the city lights twinkled behind us, I couldn't help but feel a sense of peace. For the first time in a long while, the future felt bright.

(Alliance Forged in Ice)

The next morning was unusually serene, a stark contrast to the chaotic days that had preceded it. The air was crisp and cold, carrying with it the faint hum of activity from both Elorans and the newly awakened denizens of the ancient city. And I stood at the edge of a grand courtyard within the city, its towering spires and intricate carvings shimmering under the soft light of a sun that barely peeked over the icy horizon. Then the two civilizations, separated by millennia's but now converging, were about to take the first step toward unity. And Angel approached, her violet cloak billowing slightly in the wind. And her expression was a mix of hope and apprehension. "This is a historic day," she said, her voice tinged with reverence. "I never imagined we'd see this moment." I reached for her hand, grounding her as much as myself. "Neither did I," I admitted. "But if anyone can make this alliance work, it's you." She smiled, her confidence bolstered by the words. Together, we turned to face the gathering crowd—a mix of Elorans, the research team, and the enigmatic figures from the ancient city.

Then the central plaza had been transformed into a ceremonial space. Banners bearing the symbols of Elora and the ancient city fluttered in the cold breeze, and their colors vibrant against the stark white of the surrounding ice. And at the heart of the plaza stood a massive table carved from crystal-like material, glowing faintly with an inner light. Seated at one end was the High Guardian of Elora, his commanding presence radiating calm and wisdom. At the other sat Kaelith, the leader of the ancient city, and his features worn by time but his eyes sharp with intelligence. Between them sat representatives from both sides, each carrying the weight of their respective histories. "We are here today," Kaelith began, his voice deep and resonant, "to forge a bond that transcends the barriers of time and isolation. For too long, we have been relics of a forgotten era, but with your arrival"—their gaze shifted to Angel and then to me—"we see a chance to step into the light once more." Then Angel rose from her seat, her posture regal yet approachable. "And we, the people of Elora, welcome this union with open hearts. And together, we can build a future that honors our pasts while embracing the possibilities ahead."

And as the day progressed, the two civilizations engaged in discussions about how their alliance would take shape. Then the Elorans brought their advanced technologies and harmonious philosophies to the table, while the people of the ancient city shared their deep knowledge of the Earth's history and their mastery over the elements. And I watched as Sarah and Kaelith from our team contributed ideas as well, suggesting ways to blend the strengths of both civilizations. "This isn't just about survival," Sarah said, her tone firm. "It's about thriving together. We've seen what isolation can do. It's time to move beyond it." Her words resonated deeply, earning nods of agreement from both sides.

Then during a break in the discussions, Angel and I joined Kaelith for a tour of the ancient city. The architecture was breathtaking, a seamless blend of nature and technology. Buildings carved into the ice seemed to pulse with a gentle energy, while pathways lined with glowing orbs guided the way. "This city was once the heart of a thriving civilization," Kaelith explained. "But when the ice claimed the land, we were forced to retreat and preserve what we could. But your arrival has awakened something in us—a reminder of who we once were and who we can be again." Then Angel placed a hand on Kaelith's arm, her expression earnest. "We will ensure that your legacy lives on. Together, we can create something even greater."

And as the sun dipped lower in the sky, the gathering reconvened. The High Guardian and Kaelith stood before the assembled crowd, and their hands joined in a symbolic gesture of unity. "With this alliance," the High Guardian declared, "we pledge to support one another, to share our knowledge and resources, and to protect the balance of this world." Then the crowd erupted into cheers, the sound echoing through the icy expanse. I felt a swell of pride and hope as I looked at Angel, her eyes shining with determination.

Then later that evening, as the celebrations continued, Angel and I found a quiet spot overlooking the city. And the glow of the lights below was mesmerizing, a testament to what could be achieved when people came together. "This feels like the beginning of something incredible," I said, pulling her closer. "It is," she replied, resting her head on my shoulder. "And it's because of you, Larry. Your courage, your heart... You've changed everything." I shook my head, a soft laugh escaping me. "I think we all played a part. But I won't lie—it feels good to know we've made a difference."

Then as we sat there, watching the celebrations unfold, I couldn't help but feel a sense of peace. For the first time in what felt like forever, the future seemed bright. As the alliance forged between the Elorans and the Ancient City began with hope, but hope alone was not enough. It required work, understanding, and the delicate weaving of trust across generations of isolation. Watching this process unfold was like witnessing the careful nurturing of a fragile seedling. With time, effort, and collaboration, that seedling grew into a thriving garden, where two civilizations flourished as one. And Angel and I were at the heart of this transformation, serving as a bridge between two worlds—hers and theirs. And each day brought new challenges, new triumphs, and a deeper respect for the resilience of both cultures.

Then the first sign of the alliance's strength was in the exchange of knowledge. Then the Elorans, with their advanced technology and philosophies, were eager to share their discoveries with the Ancient City. The latter, in turn, revealed their long-hidden secrets, including the workings of their energy systems, powered by the ice itself. I vividly remember the first demonstration of this exchange. The great hall of the Ancient City was filled with representatives from both sides. Then the Elorans showcased a compact device that could heal wounds using light frequencies—a marvel even to the technologically advanced city-dwellers. In response, the Ancient City revealed their method of harnessing geothermal energy from beneath the ice to sustain life in the most extreme conditions. "These are more than just tools," Kaelith, the leader of the Ancient City, said during one meeting. "They are extensions of our way of life. To share them is to share who we are." Angel was quick to respond. "And we honor that. Your history and wisdom are treasures we will protect." I couldn't help but feel proud as I watched the exchange, knowing how far we had come from the days of initial suspicion and hesitation.

Then one of the most remarkable changes was the physical transformation of the Ancient City. Then with the Elorans' help, the city began to expand. Bridges of shimmering ice and metal were constructed, connecting once-isolated districts. New habitats were built to house the growing population, including researchers from our team who had chosen to stay behind. I often joined the teams working on these projects, marveling at how seamlessly the two civilizations blended their architectural styles. Eloran structures, sleek and angular, intertwined with the organic, flowing designs of the Ancient City. Then one evening, as the sun dipped below the horizon, casting a golden glow over the icy expanse, I found myself standing on one of these new bridges with Angel. She looked out over the city, her expression contemplative. "They've made this their home," she said softly. "They have," I replied. "And it's because of you, Angel. You've shown them that there's more to life than what they knew before." She smiled, her eyes meeting mine. "We've all done this together, Larry. This city isn't just theirs or ours—it's a testament to what we can achieve when we trust each other."

Then another cornerstone of the growing alliance was the cultural exchange between the two civilizations. Festivals, art exhibitions, and shared meals became common occurrences. And one festival stood out in my memory. And it was held in the heart of the Ancient City, where a grand plaza was transformed into a celebration of unity. Then Eloran music, ethereal and melodic, blended with the deep, resonant chants of the Ancient City's inhabitants. Dancers from both cultures performed together, their movements telling stories of resilience and hope.

Angel and I stood at the edge of the crowd, our hands intertwined. "This is what it means to be united," she said. "It's beautiful," I agreed.

So of course, the path to unity wasn't without its challenges. Differences in language, customs, and priorities somethings led to misunderstandings. But each time, those involved were quick to resolve the issues through open dialogue and mutual respect. And one particular incident tested the alliance's strength. A group from the Ancient City discovered that some Eloran machinery was affecting the delicate ecosystem beneath the ice. Tensions flared, with accusations of carelessness on both sides. Then Angel stepped in, her voice calm yet firm. "We are not here to harm," she said during a heated meeting. "We are here to build. Let's find a solution together." Through collaboration, then the issue was resolved, and the alliance emerged stronger for it. And as I sat one evening, writing in the journal I had kept since arriving on the ice, I reflected on how much had changed. And now the Ancient City, that was once a ghost town, was alive with activity. And the Elorans, who had lived in isolation for so long, were now thriving alongside their new allies. Then Angel entered the room, her presence a comforting warmth in the cold night. She glanced at my journal and smiled. "Writing another epic entry?" "Something like that," I replied, grinning. She sat beside me, resting her head on my shoulder. "I hope you're capturing the truth of it all—the struggles, the triumphs, and the love that made it all possible." I kissed her forehead. "Every word."

(Reflections of the Heart)

The next day I noticed that the research station was quieter than usual. The hum of machinery and occasional clatter of equipment still punctuated the air, but there was a calmness that hadn't been there before. It felt like the world itself was holding its breath, waiting for what came next. For us, it was a time to pause and reflect—a rare chance to look back on everything we had experienced before stepping into the unknown again. I sat in the station's common room, staring at the old leather-bound journal that had accompanied me throughout this journey. Its pages were filled with stories, sketches, and moments that now seemed like a dream. Across from me, Angel was leaning against the large observation window, gazing out at the vast, icy expanse. Her silhouette was framed by the soft glow of the setting sun, casting a golden hue over her serene expression. "What's on your mind?" I asked, closing the journal and walking over to her. She turned, her lips curving into a gentle smile. "Everything," she said. "It's strange, isn't it? How life can change so much in such a short time. I never thought I'd leave Elora, let alone find myself here, preparing to go to a world I've only read about in ancient records." I reached out, taking her hand in mine. "And I never thought I'd find someone like you out here. Funny how the universe works."

Then later that evening, the entire team gathered in the station's main hall, a spacious room with walls adorned with maps, photos, and artifacts from our expeditions. And a fire crackled in the old iron stove, and its warmth a welcome contrast to the biting cold outside. Then Dr. Harrison, our team leader, stood at the head of the table and his usual stoic demeanor had softened, and there was a glint of emotion in his eyes. "Before we pack up and head back, I think it's only right to acknowledge what we've achieved—and what we've overcome." He gestured toward the table, where each of us had placed something that represented our journey. For me, it was a piece of carved ice I had taken from the Ancient City—a small, crystalline artifact that shimmered with a light I still couldn't fully explain. Angel's contribution was a woven bracelet made of threads from Eloran fabric. "A reminder of where I come from," she said when she placed it on the table. Then as the night wore on, we shared stories. Tales of the first days on the ice, our discovery of Elora, the adversaries we had faced, and the alliances we had forged. Laughter mixed with moments of solemn silence as we recounted the challenges that had tested us and the bonds that had kept us strong. "Do you remember that first storm we faced?" Dr. Dr. Harrison said, chuckling. "I was convinced we wouldn't make it." "And yet here we are," I replied. "Not just surviving—but thriving."

Then as time passed the next morning I noticed that the station buzzed with activity as we prepared for our journey back to Europe. Crates of samples and equipment were carefully packed, while personal belongings were gathered and secured. Then Angel walked through the halls with a mix of curiosity and wonder, stopping to examine every detail. And she had spent so much time in Elora and the wilderness that the research station was still somewhat of a mystery to her. "This place is so... practical," she said, running her fingers along the cold steel walls. "It's not as beautiful as Elora, I'll give you that," I said, laughing. "But it's home in its own way." She turned to me, her expression thoughtful. "Do you think your world will accept me, Larry? Will they see me as you do?" I stepped closer, placing my hands on her shoulders. "Angel, they'd be fools not to. You've changed my life—our lives. And if they can't see how amazing you are, that's their loss." Her eyes glistened with unshed tears, and she nodded. "I just hope I can bring something meaningful to your world, as you've brought to mine."

So as the sun began to dip below the horizon, casting long shadows across the station, the team gathered one last time outside. And the cold bit at my skin, but I barely felt it as I stood beside Angel, because her warmth grounding me. "We've seen things no one else on this planet has seen," Dr. Harrison said, his voice carrying across the frozen expanse. "We've forged alliances, uncovered secrets, and faced dangers we couldn't have imagined. And now, we bring those experiences back with us—not just as knowledge, but as a part of who we are." Then the team nodded, their expressions a mix of pride and anticipation. Then as the stars began to appear in the darkening sky, Angel leaned closer to me. "Are you ready for what comes next?" I looked at her, my heart swelling with a mixture of love and determination. "With you by my side, I can face anything." And in that moment, surrounded by the people who had become my family and the woman who had become my world, I felt a deep sense of peace. Whatever lay ahead—on the ice or beyond—I knew we were ready to face it together.

Then on the next day the steady hum of the airplane's engines filled the cabin, a comforting white noise that contrasted with the whirlwind of thoughts running through my mind. It had been months since I'd set foot on a commercial airplane, and yet, here I was again—this time, heading back to Europe, but with a group of people who felt more like family than colleagues. And Angel, the love of my life, sitting beside me. Angel was gazing out the window, her wide eyes taking in the expanse of clouds and endless blue sky. I couldn't help but smile as I watched her, her curiosity and wonder as vibrant as ever. "Hard to believe we're flying through the sky, isn't it?" I asked her. She turned to me, her lips curving into a smile. "It's like something out of a dream. In Elora, we have stories about the skies, but to actually be here, above the clouds... it feels magical." Her awe was contagious, making me see the experience of flight in a new light. It was easy to take things like this for granted, but through Angel's eyes, the mundane became extraordinary.

And the team was spread throughout the cabin, most of them engrossed in books, headphones, or quietly chatting. And Dr. Harrison was two rows ahead, poring over notes in his leather-bound journal, as if trying to capture every detail of the expedition before the memories faded. Sarah sat next to him, eyes closed, her head resting against the seat. She had been the one to suggest that we take a commercial flight instead of arranging for private transport, saying, "We need a taste of normalcy after everything we've been through." And as for me, normalcy seemed like a distant concept. And the events of the past few months—discovering Elora, battling the adversaries, and forging alliances that could change the course of history—had redefined what normal meant to me. "Larry," Angel said softly, breaking me out of my thoughts. "Yeah?" "Do you think they'll understand? The people on your side of the world?" Her voice was tinged with uncertainty, her fingers nervously toying with the edge of the airline blanket. Then I reached over and took her hand. "It won't be easy," I admitted. "But you have us. We'll make them see. And besides, you've already won over the toughest crowd there is—us." That earned me a soft laugh, and she leaned her head against my shoulder.

Then midway through the flight, a stewardess came by with trays of food. Angel examined her meal with an amused curiosity, tilting her head as she poked at the small compartments of pre-packaged vegetables, rice, and chicken. "This is food?" she asked, lifting a tiny butter packet. "It's airplane food," I explained with a chuckle. "Not exactly fine dining, but it'll keep us going." She nodded, taking a tentative bite before breaking into a wide grin. "It's different. But I like it." And as we ate, conversations began to flow among the team. Dr. Harrison leaned across the aisle to talk about the logistics of presenting our findings to the European research council. Sarah chimed in, her tone more relaxed than I'd heard in weeks. "We're not just presenting research," she said. "We're presenting a new chapter of human history." Angel listened intently, her interest piqued by the prospect of sharing Elora's story with the world. "Your people will know the truth," she said, her voice filled with quiet determination. "They will see that we are not so different."

And as the cabin lights dimmed and the plane settled into the long stretch of its journey, I found myself staring out into the night sky. And Angel had drifted off, her head resting on my shoulder, and the gentle rise and fall of her breathing was a soothing rhythm against the backdrop of the engine's drone. I thought back to the first flight that had brought me to Antarctica. I had been so full of ambition, so determined to prove myself. Now, I was leaving with more than I ever could have imagined—discoveries that would reshape history, alliances that could redefine our understanding of the world, and a love that felt as boundless as the sky itself. And looking around the cabin, I could see that I wasn't the only one lost in thought. As each member of the team carried their own memories, their own reflections of the journey we had shared. Dr. Harrison had a faraway look in his eyes, likely planning the next steps for our research. And Sarah was quietly sketching in a notebook, something she had taken up during our time in Elora. And even the usually talkative Drew was uncharacteristically quiet, his gaze fixed on the screen in front of him.

Then as the first light of dawn began to creep over the horizon, casting a soft glow over the clouds, the captain's voice crackled over the intercom, announcing that we were beginning our descent. And Angel stirred, her eyes fluttering open as she stretched and looked out the window. "Is that your world?" she asked, her voice hushed. "That's Europe," I said, my heart swelling with anticipation and a touch of anxiety. "It's home." She nodded, her expression a mixture of excitement and resolve. "Then let's go," she said. "Let's show them what we've found." Then as the plane began its slow descent, I reached over and took her hand once more. No matter what challenges lay ahead, I knew we would face them together.

(The Golden Age)

Then after some hours when the plane touched down in Europe, the weight of the journey we had undertaken pressed heavily on my chest. I looked out at the runway, the bustling airport a stark contrast to the icy wilderness we had left behind. And it felt surreal, almost as though we were stepping from one reality into another. And Angel, seated beside me, seemed equally awed and apprehensive, her fingers curling around the armrest of her seat. "This is it," I said, offering her a reassuring smile. "The world's about to change." Angel glanced at me, her eyes filled with determination. "It's not just the world. It's the people, the future. Everything." I nodded, knowing she was right. What we had experienced—what we had survived—wasn't just an adventure. It was the beginning of something far greater than any of us could have imagined.

And the drive to the European Research Council headquarters was quiet, the team subdued as we traveled through the city. Tall, modern buildings loomed over us, but to Angel, every sight seemed extraordinary. "These structures," she murmured, her gaze lingering on a glass skyscraper. "They're beautiful. Different from what we build, but still... beautiful." I watched her, marveling at how she could find wonder in everything. It reminded me of the way I had felt when I first laid eyes on Elora, its spires reaching toward the heavens, its streets brimming with life and light. Then by the time we arrived at the council building, a crowd had already gathered. News of our return had spread, and the public was eager to hear about our findings. Cameras flashed, reporters shouted questions, and for a moment, I felt overwhelmed by the sheer scale of it all. Angel's hand found mine, grounding me. "We'll face this together," she said softly.

Then as we entered inside the grand auditorium, the lights dimmed as Dr. Meyers took to the stage. He began with a summary of our findings—scientific, geological, and historical—but the real moment came when Angel stepped forward. Clad in a simple yet elegant dress she had chosen for the occasion, she radiated a quiet confidence. Then the room fell silent as she began to speak. "I am Angel," she said, her voice steady. "A daughter of Elora, a city hidden beyond the ice and my people have lived in harmony with the land for generations, but we are not the first. Beneath the ice lies a history far older than my kind—civilizations that thrived long before your own. This is not a story of separation but of connection. It is time for us to reunite." Her words hung in the air, resonating with a power I hadn't anticipated. She spoke of the alliances we had forged, the dangers we had faced, and the shared potential for a brighter future. And as she spoke, I could see the skepticism in the room begin to melt away, replaced by a cautious hope.

And the days that followed were a blur of meetings, negotiations, and collaborations. Governments from around the world convened, their representatives pouring over the data we had brought back. Videos and photographs of Elora and the ancient city played on screens, captivating audiences and sparking a global fascination. And Angel was at the center of it all, her eloquence and grace winning over even the most hardened skeptics. She answered questions with patience, explained Elora's ways of life, and emphasized the need for unity. "It's not about who came first," she told a group of dignitaries one afternoon. "It's about who comes together now. Our histories are intertwined. Our futures should be too."

Then within weeks, treaties were drafted, alliances formed. The ancient city's leaders, revitalized by their newfound connection to the outside world, worked closely with Earth's scientists and engineers. Knowledge flowed freely between Elora and the surface world, sparking advancements in medicine, energy, and environmental preservation. And for the first time in centuries, humanity seemed to be moving toward a shared purpose. Borders became less significant as nations collaborated on projects that benefited the planet as a whole. Then the once-fragmented world began to heal, its people inspired by the unity they had witnessed in Antarctica.

And amidst the whirlwind of progress, Angel and I found moments of quiet reflection. Standing on the balcony of a Parisian hotel one evening, we looked out over the city, its lights twinkling like stars. "This is what I hoped for," she said softly. "To see your world, to share ours, and to find a way forward together." I wrapped an arm around her shoulders, pulling her close. "You've done more than that, Angel. You've shown everyone what's possible when we let go of fear and embrace hope." She smiled, her eyes glistening with unshed tears. "I couldn't have done it without you."

So as the months turned into years, the alliance between Earth, Elora, and the ancient city only grew stronger. Technological marvels emerged, inspired by the ingenuity of all three civilizations. Environmental restoration projects revitalized areas once thought lost. Education and cultural exchanges flourished, creating a generation that saw itself as part of a global—and interstellar—community. And through it all, Angel and I continued our journey together. We became ambassadors of this new era, traveling between worlds, sharing stories, and reminding everyone of the power of unity. And the ice had once been a barrier, a symbol of isolation and mystery. But now, it was a bridge—a connection between past and future, between Earth and Elora, between hope and possibility.

Then a few years later after Angel came back to Europe with me the sunlight streamed through the windows of our home, casting a warm glow over the room. I sat on the couch, watching as my two children, Mira and Caleb, played together on the floor. Mira, our eldest at six years old, was a spitting image of Angel—her hair shimmering with a faint, otherworldly luster, and her eyes carrying the same luminous depth. Caleb, just four, had my darker complexion but a mischievous grin that belonged entirely to him. And as Angel walked into the room, her presence still as mesmerizing as the day I met her. She held a tray with cups of tea, her movements graceful and deliberate. "You're staring," she teased, setting the tray down beside me. "Can you blame me?" I replied with a smile, pulling her into a gentle embrace. "Seven years, Angel. Seven years since everything changed, and it still feels like a dream." She rested her head on my shoulder, watching our children with an expression of serene contentment. "It's not a dream, Larry. It's the life we fought for."

And the world outside our home had undergone a transformation just as profound as our own lives. Cities flourished with technologies once thought to belong only to science fiction. Sleek, sustainable energy sources powered entire continents, while advanced medicine had eradicated many diseases that once plagued humanity. Eloran designs blended seamlessly with Earth's architecture. Buildings soared higher than ever, their surfaces shimmering with living metal that absorbed sunlight and purified the air. Transport systems spanned continents and oceans, and even extended into space. And the Ancient City, now fully reawakened, stood as a testament to the power of unity. It had become a hub of innovation and collaboration, drawing scientists, artists, and visionaries from all over the world and Elora. And Angel and I had become symbols of this new era, though we had long since stepped back from the spotlight. We preferred the quieter moments, like these, surrounded by family and the simple joys of life.

"Daddy," Mira called, pulling me from my thoughts. She held up a holographic globe, a gift from her Eloran grandparents. "Where's Elora?" I knelt beside her, tapping the globe's surface. The image zoomed in on Antarctica, revealing the sprawling cities hidden beneath the ice. "Here," I said, pointing. "This is where Mommy's from." Mira's eyes widened. "And the Ancient City? Is that here too?" "It is," Angel chimed in, sitting beside us. She traced a finger along the map, showing Mira where the Ancient City lay. "It's where your father and I learned so much about our histories. And where we started dreaming about the future." Mira's brow furrowed in thought. "Can we go there someday?" Angel and I exchanged a smile. "One day," I promised. "When you're a little older."

So now our lives weren't just confined to Earth anymore. Space travel had become as routine as flying once was, with Elorans and humans traveling between worlds for work, education, and exploration. The alliance between Earth, Elora, and the Ancient City had blossomed into something even greater—a planetary community. Then Caleb's voice broke through my thoughts. "Daddy, can we go to the moon too?" Angel laughed, her musical voice filling the room. "Not today, little one. But maybe someday." I ruffled Caleb's hair, marveling at his boundless imagination. "You know," I said, "when I was your age, I never even dreamed of going to Antarctica, let alone the moon or Elora." "Then you must have been a boring kid," Caleb replied with a grin. Angel and I burst into laughter, and even Mira giggled at her brother's audacity.

Then that evening, after the children had gone to bed, Angel and I sat together on the balcony. And the city lights stretched out before us, a mixture of Earth and Eloran designs that symbolized everything we had worked for. "Do you ever think about those days on the ice?" Angel asked softly. "Every day," I admitted. "It's hard to believe how far we've come—from the blizzards and adversaries to this." She reached for my hand, her fingers intertwining with mine. "We made it, Larry. All of us. The Guardians, the Ancient City, Elora, Earth... and us." I kissed her forehead, my heart swelling with gratitude and love. "And we'll keep going. For Mira, for Caleb, for everyone." Then Angel nodded, her eyes shining with determination. "The golden age isn't just about the technology or the peace. It's about the connections we've built and the bonds we've forged. That's what will carry us forward." And as the stars twinkled above us, I couldn't help but feel a profound sense of fulfillment. Our journey wasn't over, but for the first time, it felt like we were truly home. And Together, Angel and I watched the city below, dreaming of the future not just for ourselves but for our children and the world they would inherit—a world united by love, hope, and the indomitable spirit of humanity.

www.ingramcontent.com/pod-product-compliance
Lightning Source LLC
Chambersburg PA
CBHW030345030726
47499CB00003B/907